COUNTDOWN

Acclaim for Julie Cannon's Fiction

In *Smoke and Fire*…"Cannon skillfully draws out the honest emotion and growing chemistry between her heroines, a slow burn that feels like constant foreplay leading to a spectacular climax. Though Brady is almost too good to be true, she's the perfect match for Nicole. Every scene they share leaps off the page, making this a sweet, hot, memorable read."—*Publishers Weekly*

Breaker's Passion is…"an exceptionally hot romance in an exceptionally romantic setting. …Cannon has become known for her well-drawn characters and well-written love scenes."—*Just About Write*

In *Power Play*…"Cannon gives her readers a high stakes game full of passion, humor, and incredible sex."—*Just About Write*

About *Heartland*…"There's nothing coy about the passion of these unalike dykes—it ignites at first encounter and never abates. …Cannon's well-constructed novel conveys more complexity of character and less overwrought melodrama than most stories in the crowded genre of lesbian-love-against-all-odds—a definite plus."—Richard Labonte, *Book Marks*

"Cannon has given her readers a novel rich in plot and rich in character development. Her vivid scenes touch our imaginations as her hot sex scenes touch us in many other areas. *Uncharted Passage* is a great read."—*Just About Write*

About *Just Business*…"Julie Cannon's novels just keep getting better and better! This is a delightful tale that completely engages the reader. It's a must read romance!"—*Just About Write*

"Great plot, unusual twist and wonderful women. …[*I Remember*] is an inspired romance with extremely hot sex scenes and delightful passion."—*Lesbian Reading Room*

Visit us at www.boldstrokesbooks.com

By the Author

Come and Get Me

Heart 2 Heart

Heartland

Uncharted Passage

Just Business

Power Play

Descent

Breakers Passion

Rescue Me

I Remember

Smoke and Fire

Because of You

Countdown

COUNTDOWN

by

Julie Cannon

2015

Credits

Editor: Shelley Thrasher
Production Design: Susan Ramundo
Cover Design By Sheri (graphicartist2020@hotmail.com)

Dedication

To my mom—
For all the nights we stayed up late and got up
well before the sun to watch the astronauts on TV.

CHAPTER ONE

T-minus 01day:19hours:41minutes:07seconds

"Houston, we have a problem."

Andrea sat up completely disoriented; the ringing pierced the night stillness like a whistle in a church. Her breathing was fast, a bead of sweat dripped down the side of her face, and her hand shook as she turned off her alarm clock. Swinging her feet over the side of the bed, she dropped her head into her hands and ran her hands through her hair, willing herself to regain control.

The nightmare was coming more frequently now as the launch date drew closer. The fact that her alarm tone mimicked the ringing of a telephone didn't help her nerves, but only that sound was guaranteed to wake her from a deep sleep.

Taking several deep breaths and forcing herself to breathe more evenly, Andrea walked into the bathroom, her legs a little shaky. She studied herself critically in the mirror as she waited for the shower water to heat. She'd lost weight; the stress of the last month was evident in her protruding rib cage, the dark circles more prominent under her eyes.

This will not do, she thought. I am the flight director for STS 1742. I am in command of the first mission to land a man on the moon in more than forty years. The success or failure of this mission will determine the future of space exploration to Mars.

I cannot show any sign that I am not in complete control and completely confident in its success.

A little more concealer and a few high-protein shakes during the day would hopefully remedy what she was looking at. Twenty minutes later she locked the door behind her, tossed her briefcase into the backseat, and backed out of her garage.

With the exception of a lone jogger and her neighbor, out for his customary walk with his Great Dane, she didn't see another person until she turned the corner onto South Washington Avenue. She'd chosen to live in Clear Lake City, a suburb southwest of Houston, Texas, because it was within easy driving distance to and from NASA. The city itself had close to two hundred thousand people, which swelled in the months preceding a scheduled flight and shrank in the months after it. The humidity was suffocating for most of the year, but during a few months it was simply tolerable. She'd grown up in Houston and learned long ago to just bear through the weather.

Driving almost on autopilot, Andrea reviewed her mental checklist for her day, the final day before liftoff. She had meetings with each lead mission specialist, the flight controller, and the head of NASA, and she had one last visit with the seven astronauts entrusted to her care. At some point tonight she needed to get a few hours of sleep, which was in direct conflict with her natural instinct to remain on-site and micromanage every last-minute detail.

Admittedly she was a control freak. And because she knew it, she used it her advantage and had learned over the past few years to let go of some things—at least on the surface. Her boss and coworkers had no idea that she followed them to ensure they had completed everything as required. This was her mission, and nothing could or would go wrong. Not only was this her first mission as the director, but everyone associated with this mission counted on her, depended on her to make the flight a success.

She passed Captain Roy's Bait and Tackle on her right, and a few hundred yards later she noticed the sign on the marque at Pinto's Lounge that read FRI NITE UN4SAKN. Andrea had no idea if that was a band or a drink. The lights in the parking lot of DaVinci Tattoo and Piercing Parlor were her next markers. Traffic picked up as she passed streets with names like Saturn Lane, Gemini Street, Space Center Blvd, and Moonrock Drive. The area was riddled with space-related names, indicating that without a doubt she was within a few miles of the most famous space center in the world.

She made a sweeping right turn onto NASA Parkway, which took her over Cow Bayou to the main gate. Phillip, the guard at the gate, greeted her as he had almost every day. He looked at the sticker on the left front bumper of her car and gave her badge more than a thorough once-over. Then he checked something on a list on his clipboard before signaling his partner to open the gate. Even though she'd passed through this gate almost every day for the past twelve years, he never failed to check her clearance. A friendly face was not an authorization to enter this secured facility.

As she drove through the gate, she noted that the view before her was still breathtaking. The sun had not yet split the sky from dark to light, and the lights on the buildings and around the perimeter made the view even more spectacular. She never lost the rush when the sight came into view. To her right a large digital clock with red numbers slowly counted down the time remaining until liftoff.

CHAPTER TWO

T-minus 01:18:12:52

The parking lot was full, a testament to the increasing number of people who had been working twenty-four hours a day for the last several weeks in preparation for the flight. Andrea parked her car next to a beat-up Ford F-150 pickup truck, its passenger-side mirror taped to the door with standard gray duct tape. Flight Commander Jason Albert had insisted on including at least five rolls of the heavy tape, saying they could use it for everything from repairing a torn hem to securing the wing on an airplane. Andrea was surprised he didn't ask to include some bailing wire in the payload as well.

Andrea slid her card key in and out of the card reader to the right of the thick, high-security entrance door. A loud whoosh greeted her as the doors slid open, and she stepped inside. She set her briefcase on the conveyer belt for its run through the X-ray machine and stepped into the virtual scanner for the daily peek under her clothes. Getting the all-clear signal, she badged in through one more set of double doors and walked down the hall toward the elevator to her office.

She knew the two men who were already waiting for the elevator, and they exchanged pleasantries. Seven more of her fellow NASA employees joined them, their badges displaying their photo, name, and department. Andrea barely heard the ding of the arriving car, its sound drowned out by the conversation around her. One of the men must have been relatively new because he commented on the confusing maze of halls that made up the Mission Control Center.

A little more than three years ago, after Andrea was named as flight director, her sister, Beth, had read the description of the space center from Wikipedia. They'd been seated in a corner booth at McDougal's, their favorite burger joint. It had been a popular location to hang out after class in high school, and both she and Beth had been there more times than she could count, including many of them with dates. Other than reupholstered seats, new tile on the floor, and several dozen coats of paint, the decor hadn't changed much in the past twenty-plus years. The waitresses still wore the same industrial-strength black dresses with white aprons. Andrea couldn't understand the white aprons—white in a burger joint with an abundance of ketchup, mustard, and hot sauce? Their uniforms were topped off, literally, with ridiculous black bows secured to the top of their head with bobby pins, or who knows what else.

In her booming, theatrical voice Beth recited, "The Johnson Space Center is the National Aeronautics and Space Administration's center for human spaceflight training, research, and flight control. The center consists of a complex of one hundred buildings constructed on over sixteen hundred acres and was nicknamed 'Space City' in 1967. The Flight Director, also known as 'Flight,' has the overall responsibility for missions and payload operations and for all decisions regarding safe, expedient flight. The Mission Operations Director, or MOD," Beth spelled out the letters, "is a representative of the senior management chain at the JSC and is there to help the flight director make those decisions that have no safety-of-flight consequences, but may have cost or public perception consequences. The MOD cannot overrule the Flight Director during a mission."

"Thanks," Andrea said, stabbing her lettuce with her fork. *"But you know what I do. Why all the fuss?"* She'd been surprised when Beth had called and invited her for lunch. They usually kept in touch by phone or, when their lives got really hectic, texts. Occasionally they'd do a family barbecue.

"Because it is a big deal, little sister. It's not every day you're named as the top dog on a space mission. A space mission, for crying out loud," she said, shaking her head. *"I still can't believe it. Hey, do you remember when we used to watch reruns of* Lost in Space *on that oldies TV station? 'Warning Will Robinson, warning,'"* Beth said, moving her stiff arms up and down, mimicking the robot on the 1960s TV show. They both laughed.

"All I wanted was to be Major Don West, the pilot of the Jupiter 2," Andrea said wistfully. She'd dreamed of being an astronaut, but her vision didn't share the same dream. Without her contacts she could barely see her fingers in front of her face.

"That's because you had the hots for the daughter. What was her name?" Beth asked, tapping her fork on her plate like the motion would make her remember the character's name.

"Judy, and I did not have the hots for her," Andrea said.

"You just didn't know you had the hots for her yet," Beth said in her I'm-the-older-therefore-smarter-twin tone. *"We had it figured out long before you did. I, for one, am sure glad you've increased your self-awareness since then."*

Andrea reflected on that comment while they finished the order of onion rings they were sharing. *"I'll never forget my coming-out conversation with Mom. Remember? I was twenty-three, sitting in the living room of the house I grew up in when I manage to have that awkward discussion."*

"I can just picture it," Beth said, grinning. *"Mom was at the sink probably peeling potatoes for dinner or shucking green beans, and you were sitting on that rickety bar stool wringing your hands like you do when you're nervous."*

That was creepy because that was exactly how it happened. *"I practiced what I was going to tell her for days, but when the time came, my mind went blank. Somehow I was able to say, 'Mom, uh, there's something I need to talk to you about.' My hands were damp and clammy, and I kept wiping them on my pants. My mouth was dry and my voice quivered, and I felt like I was going to throw up. I was a mess. And when she said 'You're pregnant,' I knew the conversation was going to be more difficult than I'd imagined."*

Both she and Beth laughed, and Andrea took another bite of her ring. "All I could say was 'No, I'm not pregnant.' Then I was a complete idiot and said, 'As a matter of fact, Mom, I'll never have to worry about getting pregnant when I have sex.' That was the stupidest thing I could have said. I didn't want to make it about sex. Jeez, not with Mom," she added with distaste.

"Then Mom looked at me like I'd just spoken in a foreign language. She asked me what in the hell I was talking about."

"That's Mom," Beth said chuckling. "Never one to mince words. Typical high-school math teacher."

Andrea nodded. "Yeah. Mom's so linear and not very good with abstract concepts or subtleties. I think that's what worried me the most—knowing I'd have to spell things out for her. Obviously that was one of those times.

"So I just came out with it. 'I'm a lesbian, Mom.' Just that simple. She cocked her head in that way she does when she's thinking something through."

This time Beth nodded.

"And then with a straight face Mom said, 'And Beth is a Republican and we still love her. What's your point?' I about fell out of the chair. And that was the end of that conversation."

"God, Andi, every time you tell that story I can hear Mom's voice. I would have loved to have been a fly on the wall for that conversation."

"She was so cool about it. I knew she wouldn't disown me, but I was scared to death. And my big news turned out to be almost a nonevent, like everyone had known about me before I did."

Andrea shook her head, embarrassed by how silly she'd been, and returned the conversation to her early fascination with space travel. "*My favorite was* The Jetsons. *I thought it was the coolest thing that George Jetson would fly around Orbit City in his little spaceship.*"

"*And go to work at Spacely Sprockets,*" *Beth added excitedly.* "*God. Watching Saturday-morning cartoons was one of best parts of the good old days, wasn't it?*"

"*Jesus, Beth. You're not even forty. You sound like your life is over.*"

"*With a husband of seventeen years, three kids, one of which has yet to sleep through the night, a mortgage, a minivan, two dogs, and four hamsters, sometimes I feel like it is.*"

Andrea knew Beth loved her family and was only talking smack. "*I told you not to buy that minivan. It just screams b-o-r-i-n-g.*"

"*What am I supposed to drive to haul the kids, their friends, and all their crap to and from everywhere? They certainly wouldn't fit in Ken's Camry.*"

"*A Suburban.*"

"*A suburban what?*" *Beth asked before taking a bite of her spaghetti.*

"*A Chevy Suburban or a Ford Expedition,*" *she added as an afterthought.* "*Something that will hold a Scout troop and make you look like a bad-ass-mother...what?*" *Andrea asked as if she didn't know what the expression on Beth's face meant.* "*That's all I was going to say, a bad-ass mother.*" *She was lying.*

"*Well, it's too late now. I'm stuck with it for thirty-eight more payments.*"

"*Are you really happy, Beth? I mean really happy?*" *Andrea asked.*

Where did that question come from? They never talked about this kind of personal stuff. Beth obviously thought the same thing because her fork stopped halfway to her mouth before she put it back down on her plate. She wiped her mouth on her napkin.

"*Yes, Andi, I am happy. Very happy,*" *she said seriously.* "*I wouldn't trade my life for anything. Why do you ask?*"

"Just curious," Andrea said, knowing she never should have asked the question.

"Bullshit, what's going on, Andi?" Beth was the only one she allowed to call her Andi.

Beth was one of the few people who understood her probably better than anyone, including herself. And she was her best friend. "Just wondered, that's all." It was a lame excuse, but it was all she had. She had no idea why she'd asked.

"Uh-huh," Beth said, obviously not convinced. "Are you seeing anyone?"

Beth's question caught her off guard. She certainly wasn't expecting that one. "Not at the moment," she replied evasively. She couldn't remember the last time she'd had a date, and sex was a vague memory. "As you so accurately pointed out from Wikipedia, I have been a little busy lately."

"That's a convenient excuse."

"Excuse me?" Beth's statement flabbergasted Andrea. "I have the lives of seven crew members on my shoulders, plus the success of a very important mission to the moon, and you think that's an excuse for not dating?"

"Of course not. But when was the last time you had sex?"

Andrea choked on a piece of bread that suddenly got stuck in her throat. "What?"

"Sex, you know...get naked, bodies touching, lots of rubbing, touching, hand and tongues in and on hard, wet body parts. If you do it right your head blows off. Sex."

Andrea was shocked at Beth's very descriptive definition. She didn't know what to say.

"That long, huh? Okay, when was the last time you had a date?" When Andrea didn't answer she went on. "Well, how about flirted with someone?" When she still didn't answer Beth said, "Andi, you need to get a life. Or at least get laid once in a while. It does wonders for the disposition."

Finally Andrea was able to speak. "Holy shit, Beth. All I did was ask you if you were happy. How did this turn into me?"

"Because I love you. The whole family loves you, and we just want you to be happy."

"I am happy," Andrea replied.

"We want to see you with someone, Andi." Beth emphasized the word with. *Someone to share your life with, care about you, make you smile, make you blush when you think of her. That kind of happy."*

"Not everyone needs your kind of happiness, Beth."

"I'm not talking about a minivan and three kids. I'm talking about a warm body to wake up to, a pair of strong arms to hold you, someone to share your life with."

She'd expected the topics of the conversation to be benign and familial, but somehow it had turned serious in the blink of one question. She didn't want to discuss this subject. She was on the verge of professional success and couldn't afford any distractions.

"I appreciate your concern, Beth, but I'm fine. Really," she added to assuage the look of skepticism on her sister's face. *"Now tell me about that nephew of mine. What sport's draining your wallet now?"*

CHAPTER THREE

T-minus 00:00:01:08

"Flight, we have confirmation three main engines ready for ignition."

"Confirmed," Andrea replied into her headset at the status check from the booster-systems engineer. He monitored and evaluated performance of propulsion-related aspects during prelaunch and descent. He had the power to send an abort command to the spacecraft.

Her voice was steady but her heart was racing. The digital readout to her left read one minute to liftoff. The tension in her shoulders increased. Her team had trained for this for countless months, and she had prepared herself for this moment for years. But the actuality of what was about to happen under her command was almost overwhelming.

"Space shuttle now on internal power," the voice said. "Solid rocket-booster flight-data recorders are activated. Confirm handoff to *Explorer* on-board computers. *Explorer* is now in control of the countdown."

"Confirmed, *Explorer* in control," Andrea said, repeating the line she'd practiced hundreds of times in simulation. But this was no simulation.

She glanced around the room, taking in the status of every position that would monitor this mission for the next nine days. All she could see was the back of everyone's head, as their attention switched from the screen in front of them to the large video display at the front of the large room. The lights were low to enable a better view of the screen, each workstation having its own desktop lighting. With the exception of a few technicians tapping commands on their keyboards, the room was quiet.

"Firing chain is armed. T minus ten, nine, eight…"

Andrea counted down in her head along with everyone in the room. As the seconds decreased, Andrea's pulse rate increased. She swallowed and took several deep breaths.

"Three, two, one. Liftoff. We have liftoff of STS 1742 and shuttle *Explorer*, the first mission to land a man on the moon since *Apollo 17* in 1972. A new generation of space exploration has begun."

Andrea breathed a sigh of relief. The first of many, many major hurdles had been successful. The shuttle and its main booster rockets had cleared the tower.

The sight of the five-million-pound man-made machine lifting off in a cloud of flame and smoke never ceased to leave her breathless. The close-up shot of the main engine exhaust showed the mammoth machine slowly lifting off the launch platform, struggling to break the earth's gravitational pull. Seven million pounds of thrust pulled the shuttle and its engines off the ground as the seconds ticked by.

Andrea knew the intricate complexity of the pipes, pumps, engines, wiring, programming, welds, nuts, and bolts that made this sight a reality. Even if she didn't, the sight was and would forever be nothing short of awesome. "Thirty seconds into the flight, *Explorer* two miles in altitude, traveling five hundred miles per hour, carrying four-and-a-half-million pounds of hardware, eight minutes to orbit," the voice said in her ear.

Her eyes were open, but Andrea visualized everything her crew was doing at this stage of the flight. Commander Jason Albert and co-pilot Tony Douglas were checking the numerous control panels that indicated the status of every system in the multimillion-dollar taxi. Mission specialists Molly Tremain, William Daniel,

Jonathon Franklin, Kathleen Martinez, and LeAnna Wethersfield were seated behind them, and each had their own set of panels to keep an eye on.

Andrea was better acquainted with her crew than anyone else on this mission. She knew what the crew was doing at this moment but not what they were feeling. She wondered what their families were going through as they watched their husbands, fathers, wives, sisters, and sons blast into space at over two thousand miles an hour.

At one time, like most children, she had dreamed of being an astronaut. Except she was the only girl who had that dream, or at least the only one who admitted it. Her girlfriends at school had ticked off the standard professions such as doctor, lawyer, mom, and the requisite one—teacher. Her what-do-you-want-to-be-when-you-grow-up had been more consistent with that of the boys in her class. Policeman, fireman, cowboy, and astronaut. She was headed down the path of her dreams, but in addition to her awful vision, she had developed a severe case of claustrophobia that had derailed that dream. She handled one with contacts and the other with meditation, but both washed her out of any chance she had to walk on the moon.

"Three good fuel cells, Flight." Booster spoke confidently. Andrea glanced at the mission clock, then quickly to the screen. Everyone in the room held their breath as *Explorer* passed the seventy-three-second mark. This was the exact time when an O-ring failure on the right solid booster rocket had made the shuttle *Challenger* a' household name and the worst disaster in NASA history.

"One minute, fifty seconds away from solid rocket separation."

Andrea scanned the heads in the room for any sign of trouble or issue with their readouts. Everything and everyone looked exactly as they had rehearsed. She started to relax.

"Two minutes into the flight and we have solid rocket booster separation. *Explorer* is thirty-four miles in altitude and traveling approximately thirty-two hundred miles per hour."

The external mounted camera on booster number two showed a flawless separation, and the *Explorer* floated away from its taxi into space.

"*Explorer*, we are at the four-minute mark. Negative return."

"We copy, Houston. *Explorer* negative return." The reception was scratchy as Commander Albert's voice confirmed that the *Explorer* was too far away from where it had lifted off and at too high of an altitude to return to the Kennedy Space Center.

Two minutes later, Capcom announced, "Six minutes into flight at an altitude of sixty-six miles, traveling at over eleven thousand miles per hour. All systems performing normally. On course, on track for preliminary orbit in fifty-eight seconds. Standing by for main engine cutoff."

"Roger, Capcom," Andrea said, relaxing the strangling grip she held on her pen. She opened and closed her hand a few times to make the circulation move again.

"Confirm external tank separation. Congratulations, *Explorer*, a flawless flight into orbit." And it was all Andrea could do to not collapse into her chair in relief. The next milestone was landing on the moon.

❖

Andrea watched in awe as Mission Specialist Molly Tremain stepped out of the shuttle and onto the surface of the moon. Her pulse raced when Molly activated her body camera and gave everyone a front-row seat to history. The scene was eerily like the first moon walk when astronaut Neil Armstrong hopped down from the ladder on the lunar module and kicked up moon dust. Tremain's heavy boots did the same, but in this case the picture was not fuzzy but crystal clear, and her words were clipped and concise. "Houston, *Explorer* has arrived."

Every minute for the next three hours, Andrea watched as Tremain and three of her crew mates unloaded their tools and experiments from the cargo bay of the shuttle. Gravity on the moon was less than twenty percent that of the earth, and the crew bounced around the surface, reminding her of a balloon being batted around a room. The picture was a bit fuzzy but at least ten dozen times clearer than anything ever seen on previous moon walks. Several times Andrea felt her body sway, almost mimicking the movements of the crew as they bounded across the surface.

The next five days went exactly as they had trained, with no deviation in the timeline, procedure, or protocol. The crew finished their experiments on the surface, gathered up their samples, and reentered the shuttle to secure their bounty. All that was left was to lift off and begin their journey home.

CHAPTER FOUR

T-minus 13:03:42:08

"Houston, we have a problem."

Andrea dropped her pencil and sat up straighter in her chair, touching the earpiece in her left ear. She tilted her head to the side as if that would improve reception with the crew over a quarter of a million miles away.

"*Explorer*, this is Houston. Say again."

"Houston, *Explorer*, I repeat, we have a problem. The main engine ignition switch is red. I repeat, the main engine ignition light is red. Switching to secondary switch number one." The voice of Mission Commander Albert was calm.

Andrea's heart raced, and she immediately looked at the console in front of her. One red light at the upper left-hand corner of the screen winked at her. Up to this point the mission had been flawless.

The shuttle had landed within inches of the designated landing area, and the crew had completed the experiments and exploration of the moon as rehearsed. Now, four days later, it was time to come home.

"Copy that, *Explorer*. Switch to secondary ignition switch."

Andrea held her breath as she waited for the indication that the shuttle engines had fired.

"Houston, this is *Explorer*. Secondary ignition switch is red. I repeat, secondary ignition switch is red. Switching to ignition switch number three."

"Copy that, *Explorer*, switch to ignition switch number three," Capcom repeated.

Suddenly a sea of flashing red lights blinked at her, signaling nothing short of a major disaster. Quickly she scanned the room as twenty-seven mission specialists anxiously checked and double-checked their data. The constant murmur in the room that had been her companion for the past eight days was now increasing in volume as they fired questions and status reports back and forth across the room. As if on cue, every head in the room turned and looked at her. The expressions on their faces left little doubt as to the severity of the situation.

Suzanne Westfield, Andrea's second in command, spoke first without being asked. "We have failure to ignite on main engines one, two, and three." Suzanne's voice was calm, but Andrea detected a slight tremor of anxiety that only she could hear.

She nodded and turned her attention to Harrison Street, a thirty-eight year NASA veteran manning the Propulsion station, the station whose job it was to monitor the engine performance. Harrison shook his head almost imperceptibly, and Andrea's stomach dropped.

This couldn't be happening. Dread, fear, and panic were just a few of the words to describe the churning in her gut. Her brain, always operating at top capacity, had stalled to the point that she wasn't sure if she even remembered her own name. Instinct and training kicked in a split second later, and a calmness she had perfected over the years settled over her. She'd worked and trained her entire life for this mission. Failure was not an option.

The phone beside her started to ring. She and the other thirty-eight people in the room had no doubt who was on the other end. She gritted her teeth and remained calm. This was not going to happen on her watch.

CHAPTER FIVE

T-minus 10:22:48:17

"Don't answer that, baby."

The woman under her grabbed Kenner tightly and pulled her down for another searing kiss. It was good. No, it was better than good, but when had the voice of the mystery woman turned from sultry to irritating? It must have been the fourth or fifth cocktail that had changed Kenner's sense of hearing. The words of a country song floated through her head—something about how all the girls get prettier at closing time. It was obviously true that the same could be said about the number of cocktails. But that was hours ago and both had worn off.

In one respect, Kenner didn't want to get up and find her pants and phone. The opportunity to silence the woman either with her own mouth or put the woman's mouth to other uses was tempting. She definitely knew what to do with her lips and tongue and even her teeth, and Kenner's clit started throbbing again just thinking about it. But answering the call would give her an excellent exit opportunity. The night and this woman had turned out exactly how she'd envisioned it. But it was time to go.

"I'm sorry, Cheri. I have to. I don't have a choice," Kenner replied in fluid French. Digging her phone out of her back pocket, she glanced at the readout. It was a U.S. area code, but she didn't recognize the number.

"Kenner," she said abruptly, her standard greeting.

"Kenner Hutchings?"

The sound on the other end of the line had some static, but it was coming from halfway around the world. "Yes," she replied. She wanted to add "and who's this" but thought it might thwart her ability use the call as a means to escape.

"Ms. Hutchings, my name is Andrea Finley. I'm the flight director at NASA for the space shuttle *Explorer*."

Kenner shook her head, trying to encourage the wheels of recognition of what the woman said to start turning. Several things the woman said were familiar, but she was having a hard time lining them all up in the right order.

"How did you get this number?"

"Ms. Hutchings, that doesn't matter right now."

"Yes, it does, and unless you tell me right now where you got this number, I'm hanging up and will not pick up again." Kenner heard what she could only describe as an exasperated sigh. What did she say her name was again? Mandy? What the hell. It didn't matter.

"Roosevelt Poplar."

Kenner didn't know if she should be surprised or pissed. Her boss at the Quantum Group liked to name-drop and used every opportunity to flaunt the brains inside his organization. Kenner couldn't stand the politics and politicking that went on at his level. Obviously Rooster, as his employees called him—though only behind his back—had dropped her name in a circle she didn't socialize in.

"Ms. Hutchings—"

"I'm here," Kenner said. "What do you want?"

"Ms. Hutchings, is this a secure line?"

"If you mean is anyone listening over my shoulder, no. But this is my cell phone," Kenner said as she walked out of the bedroom and closed the door behind her. At least she wasn't lying to the woman on the phone.

"What did you say your name was?"

"Andrea Finley, from NASA in Houston."

"Ms. Finley, it's four in the morning. What do you want?" Kenner repeated. She didn't mean to be abrupt, but it was the middle of the night.

"Ms. Hutchings." The voice on the other end of the line paused so long Kenner thought they'd lost the connection. "We need your assistance."

"With what?"

"We have a situation, and my experts have told me you'd be able to help."

Kenner wasn't very politically astute, but she detected more than a slight hesitation in this woman's request for her help. What she did know about NASA and the government wasn't much, but she had heard they rarely looked outside their own, believing they had the solution to everything.

"What is the problem?"

"Ms. Hutchings—"

"Call me Kenner. Ms. Hutchings is my mother, and I'm nothing like her."

The woman hesitated, obvious uncomfortable being on a first-name basis. "It's something I can't really delve into over the phone."

Kenner read between the lines. What she really said was they she was on an unsecured line and something was fucked. "If you'll tell me where you are, we'll send a plane for you."

"I'm on vacation."

"Ms. Hutchings, this isn't really optional."

"Ms. Finley, no offense, but I don't work for you. I haven't had a vacation in four years, and I'm not about to cut it short to go to Houston." Kenner spoke with more than a little distaste when she said the word Houston. Houston compared to the South of France was like cubic zirconium compared to diamonds or Kobe beef to bologna.

"You're absolutely right, Ms. Hutchings. You don't work for me. But we have seven people in serious trouble, and you need to work for them."

CHAPTER SIX

T-minus 10:14:08:22

"This is horse shit," Kenner said, back in her hotel room packing her suitcase. "Complete and utter horse shit. I'm supposed to be on vacation, completely out of touch. How in the hell did Rooster even get my cell-phone number?" Kenner asked into the empty room. She preferred talking out loud instead of in her head. Something about saying the words aloud and hearing them gave her an extra perspective on things. She would often pace in her office or stand in front of her whiteboard talking to herself as she unraveled the complexity of whatever problem she was working on at the time. Some days she was so hoarse by the time she got home she soothed her parched throat with a little whiskey and a dab of honey thrown in strictly for medicinal purposes.

She was still mumbling to herself when she hailed a cab and sat back for the twenty-mile drive to the Marseille Provence Airport. Her connection in New York was several hours long, allowing an unrushed pilgrimage through customs. From there she was catching a flight to Houston. Way too many hours in a plane. She hated flying, but it was the quickest way to get from point A to point B, and she was all about speed and efficiency.

The flight attendant was particularly attentive, and Kenner knew if she wanted a little time-killing activity in the rear of the plane she could get it. She'd been a member of the mile-high club for several years, and however exciting and dangerous it was, tonight it didn't appeal to her.

The marvel of technology enabled her to Google anything and everything during the flight. She typed NASA in the search bar and in zero point three four seconds pulled up over eighty million hits. That was a ridiculous, useless way to try to figure out just what in the hell was so important that only she could fix.

Scrolling through the hits, she spotted an article in *Time* magazine on Andrea Finley. Thirty-seven years old, first female flight director, graduated summa cum laude with a Master's degree in Aeronautical Engineering from MIT. "Hmm, a fellow alumni," Kenner said quietly after reading this information. "I don't remember seeing anything that good on campus. But then again I graduated several years after Ms. Finley."

The photograph of Flight Director Finley was taken by a professional. It captured the blue of her eyes and a calm, confident attitude in the tall, thin blonde. Her arms were casually crossed across her chest, and she was leaning against a desk that could only be described as nondescript. Heaven forbid our tax dollars funded a lavish lifestyle and office décor. On a table behind her sat several models of the space shuttle and other NASA rockets.

But it was her eyes that kept drawing Kenner's attention. The directness and confidence reflected in them was simply alluring. It was ridiculous. It was just a picture, not a flesh-and-blood woman standing in front of her. But something about her appealed to Kenner. Even though she was angry her vacation had been cut short, she really wanted to know what Flight Director Finley looked like with her hair messed, preferably from Kenner's hands running through it.

Feeling the familiar tingling in her crotch reminded Kenner that she hadn't had nearly enough sex on this short vacation. But Houston was full of women. She was sure she could find a tall, sun-bronzed goddess whose body she could worship. After all, all work and no play made Kenner a very dull and cranky girl.

The article went on to talk about Flight Director Finley's commitment to the space program and how the lives of the men and women on the crew depended on her and her team to launch them into orbit and safely return. She'd been assistant flight director on seven previous flights and didn't think it was any big deal whatsoever that she was female.

"My gender has nothing to do with it," the article said, quoting her. "Did it matter that previous directors like Mitch Roberts was a single dad or that Frank Thomas had a wife and four kids or that Paul Embry was divorced? No, it didn't, and it doesn't with me either. What matters is that I've been trained to do this job, and I will do it to the best of my ability." Or the fact that I'm a lesbian, Kenner added in her head.

Even after only a short phone conversation halfway across the world, Kenner could almost hear the flight director's voice when she spoke to the reporter. Her Southern drawl was sexy but strong, stern, no-nonsense. Typical for a woman in a man's field who didn't want anyone to see her as anything other than one hundred percent professional. Kenner had been around these types of women before—the ones who downplayed the fact that they were female. Some went to such an extreme as to camouflage their natural beauty and grace so that when anyone looked at them they didn't see a woman but a professional.

Kenner always wondered what those women were like outside the office, behind the front door. And she wondered how some of them, including Andrea Finley, were behind their bedroom door as well. Kenner had the fortunate luck or skill to get the answer to that question, but something in the determined set of Ms. Finley's jaw and the direct look in her eyes said "Don't even begin to try." That door was closed, locked, and bolted tightly. What a shame, Kenner thought. Even behind the exterior seriousness, Andrea Finley was a damn fine attractive woman.

CHAPTER SEVEN

T-minus 10:14:38:04

Andrea slowed her steps as she approached the Flight Operations Director's office. Her boss, Barry Haven, was a reasonable man when things were going smoothly, but his level of calmness disappeared as the level of stress in the situation increased. Andrea didn't admire that trait in her boss or in anyone associated with any of these flights. On the contrary, the more difficult the situation was, the calmer the team needed everyone to be, especially their leader.

She rapped on the open door. "Barry?"

He motioned her in with a chubby hand. "I hope you have good news for me, because you sure do need it," he replied gruffly.

Like everyone involved with dealing with this problem, he'd been here for far too many hours. His constant five o'clock shadow now looked like a full beard, and his eyes were bloodshot. His always impeccably pressed shirt was wrinkled and his tie not in its usual tight Windsor knot around his neck. Three Styrofoam coffee cups littered his desk, and judging by the coffee stain on the side of one of the cups and the dried coffee stain on the folder underneath it, one of them had overflowed the rim hours ago.

Andrea didn't bother sitting down; her briefing would be short and to the point. She didn't bother with idle small talk in the normal course of the day, and in this situation it would have been totally out of place.

"I reached Kenner Hutchings. She was someplace in the South of France. She won't be here until early tomorrow morning."

"Shit." Barry shook his head. "I wish I could go to the fucking South of France." He rubbed his hands over his face, and Andrea could hear the scratching of his beard.

This wasn't the first time Andrea had heard her boss curse. He didn't make it a habit, but when he did, it was at an appropriate time. The first time he'd dropped the f-bomb she was shocked. She'd never heard it in the workplace—at least not in the office. She'd heard it plenty on the construction floor and the flight line, but not by anyone wearing a silk tie. And as much as she wanted to experience the freedom that cussing at a certain situation made her feel, she believed it would only undermine her credibility and refused to do so. She saved those words for the speed bag in the corner of her spare bedroom, turned weight room, and the really big words for the heavy bag that hung in the opposite corner.

"Did you tell her what we have?"

"No sir, I didn't," Andrea replied formally. "The line wasn't secure. And it's not something I really wanted to get into over the phone. That and the fact that she probably wouldn't have understood half of what I was talking about." Andrea tried to keep the resentment out of her voice.

She'd been forced to call Kenner Hutchings, a twenty-six-year-old whiz kid with a PhD in mathematics and aeronautical engineering from her alma mater MIT. From all the accounts that Andrea had read and picked up from her colleagues in their discussions of Kenner's ability, she also had a cocky attitude that rounded out the package. There would have been no point in explaining what their situation was. She wasn't a NASA engineer. She didn't know the space shuttle, or a booster rocket from a landing rover. Trying to discuss the technicalities of the situation would have been pointless and would eat up valuable time. Andrea would have to do all her briefing once Kenner arrived on site.

"You don't seem overjoyed that this…what's his name again?"

"It's a she, and her name is Kenner Hutchings."

"What kind of name is that, Kenner?"

"I have no idea, sir. Probably some family heirloom of some kind. If she can solve our problem, I don't care if she's sprouting wings and has a halo."

Barry looked at her for several moments as if trying to figure out how big her lie was. She wasn't really lying. If Kenner could solve their problem, this was where she needed to be. It just grated on Andrea that it had to be on her mission. Finally Barry saw whatever it was he was looking for and effectively dismissed her with a terse "Keep me informed." Andrea followed up with an equally terse "Yes sir," before she turned and closed the door behind her.

The scene that greeted her in the control room wasn't what she'd expected. Four people were crowded into the Medical work area that normally held one. All four heads were bent, and two of the men kept checking and rechecking the readouts in front of them. This was not good.

"What is it?" she asked Suzanne, the assistant flight director on this shift.

"Albert has a fever."

Great, Andrea thought. Just what they needed, a problem with the shuttle commander.

"What does Medical say? And don't tell me he has a fever," she said, looking over to the doctor currently manning the console that monitored everything going on, in and out of the crew's bodies.

"His temperature is one hundred and three. He's complaining of body aches and nausea."

Unbelievable. They'd rocketed seven human beings into space to walk on the moon. They had the latest, most sophisticated technology in the world, and the man in charge had the flu. Unless they solved the problem facing them, it wouldn't matter if the pilot of the four-hundred-fifty-million-dollar shuttle was too sick to fly.

Chapter Eight

T-minus 08:13:27:52

"Jesus, you'd think I was trying to get into Fort Knox or the White House or something," Kenner mumbled under her breath as she exited the visitors building. She'd been photographed, fingerprinted, and searched so thoroughly she'd commented to the security officer that maybe she should have dinner first next time. Nobody had laughed.

The same serious, burly man that had picked her up at the airport led the way through a set of impressively secure double doors. She felt like she was going into a prison instead of entering the control center of NASA. The intense security was a complete contrast to the all-American, apple-pie reputation of the space agency. I guess if the shuttle or one of the rockets fell into the wrong hands it could be very, very ugly. Let's hope I'm not around if that ever happens, she thought, and shook the image from her head.

Kenner was able to keep track of the number of right and left turns they made, and even though she had no idea where they were going, she knew she could find her way out of this maze blindfolded. This building hadn't looked this big when they drove up to it. Finally they stopped in front of yet another card-access door, but this one was guarded by a lean, mean, fighting machine wearing a U.S. Air Force uniform.

The man looked at Kenner, her badge, then back at her. He checked something on his clipboard—and what was it with that old brown clipboard? Hadn't any of these guys ever heard of the iPad? The guard nodded, Kenner swiped her badge, and the green door opened.

❖

Christ, another hall, this one painted blue. She wondered if this color code was to distinguish one from another, some sort of psychological calming effect, or maybe a team-building event and the blue team had painted this one. They stopped in front of a wooden door polished to a high gloss with the words CONFERENCE ROOM A embossed in gold letters stenciled at just about eye level. Her guide knocked twice on the door, opened it, and motioned for Kenner to enter. When she did, he closed the door behind her, leaving her in a room with nineteen men, eight women, and no introductions.

All conversation in the room stopped, and every set of eyes turned her way. She was obviously odd man out in the room and at least twenty years younger than the youngest person sitting around the table. But this sort of shit didn't intimidate Kenner in the least. She knew she was smart, very smart as a matter of fact, and she wouldn't be here if she wasn't qualified to help with whatever the hell was going on.

"Good morning," she said. "I'm Kenner Hutchings." No one at the table gave any indication of acknowledging her introduction or introducing themselves, so she started with the man to her immediate left. She stuck out her hand and said, "And you are?"

"Jack Stevens, Booster."

"Nice to meet you, Jack."

"Rob Jazinski, Medical," the next man said.

"Paul Cooler, Guidance."

The introductions continued around the room, and Kenner wondered if that was the way everyone introduced themselves around here. If so, what would she say...Kenner Hutchings, technical consultant? Problem solver? Lifesaver? Introductions finished, she poured herself a cup of coffee from the large silver urn on the side table. Between running her vacation full speed, sampling the local highlights, and flying halfway around the world, she desperately needed the caffeine, and lots of it.

Kenner didn't require a lot of sleep. When she was a child, most nights she'd stayed up later than her parents. They would insist she go to bed and Kenner had complied, but once tucked in she would turn on her flashlight, pull the covers over her head, and read, draw, or write stories in a blue, battered wire-bound notebook. Whether it was her natural body makeup or that she rarely operated at anything other than full speed, she knew her limits and she was there. A cup or three of good strong coffee would fuel her for whatever she had to face today.

The seats at both ends of the rectangle table were empty, as well as the seat next to Jack Stevens, the first man she'd introduced herself to. Not being shy in the least, she sat down on the end, leaned back in the chair, crossed her legs, and waited for whatever or whoever was going to start this meeting.

She found it interesting that these people worked together, yet there was no small talk or chatter around the table. Obviously something serious was going on; otherwise, she wouldn't be here, but they weren't even talking about that. That was odd, she thought, unless they didn't know why she was there. Not two minutes later the door opened again, and every head turned with a look of expectation on each face when Flight Director Andrea Finley walked in.

❖

The photo from the NASA website didn't do justice to the sheer power and professional magnetism that Andrea exuded when she walked into the room. Kenner was taken aback at that combination and, no matter how hard she tried to disguise it, the sheer sensuality of the woman. She was tall, Kenner guessed probably close to six feet, thinner than she appeared in her photo, with a sense of fatigue on her smooth face. Because of the way Kenner's brain worked, she observed and retained every single detail of every single thing. She'd learned how to shut this ability off; otherwise she'd go nuts.

Director Finley didn't slouch or try to compensate for her height in any way as she walked into the room and set her portfolio down at the head of the table. She made a quick glance around the room, and her eyes stopped on Kenner. Kenner's pulse raced when their eyes met, and she found it slightly hard to breathe. Feeling uncomfortable, she rose from her chair and walked toward the flight director with her hand outstretched.

"Director Finley, I'm Kenner Hutchings." She wasn't sure how her voice sounded as strong as it did in spite of the butterflies that were kick-boxing in her stomach. The director's hand was warm, her handshake firm as she introduced herself as well.

"Ms. Hutchins, thank you for coming."

Her voice was strong and deep, her Southern drawl stronger in person than it was over the telephone.

"Kenner, please," she said, and felt an odd sense of loss when Andrea removed her hand and moved to her seat at the head of the table.

"Did you meet everyone?" she asked, her outstretched hands indicating the others.

"Yes, I did, thank you. I introduced myself," Kenner said, making it clear that she was the one who'd made the introductions, not the other way around.

"All right then, let's get started." Andrea opened her portfolio, picked up her pen, and had everyone's attention.

For the next hour Andrea outlined the current status, steps that had been taken, and what was in progress in an attempt to rectify the problem. Kenner listened, not fully understanding all the technical jargon they were using. Several times Andrea was polite enough to spell some of the terms out so she could understand. It started to become very clear that there was a serious problem with the space shuttle. Holy shit. *No wonder she couldn't talk to me on the phone.*

Sitting on the opposite side of the table, Kenner admired Andrea's control of the situation and her grasp of the elements. She never once wavered, never once sat back in her chair, and continually pressed the people in the room with solutions, however farfetched, even for a possible solution. Their marching orders clear, the meeting adjourned and everyone practically fled the room, leaving Kenner and Andrea alone.

"I don't expect you to comprehend all the technicalities of the situation," Andrea said, approaching her.

"Not at this point, no," she answered. "But I will."

"There's an office for you just down the hall," Andrea informed her as she led them out of the conference room. "It's set up with access to our database, the print schematics, and the programs we use. You can start with—"

"Could you have someone show me around? You know, who does what, how it all fits together, how the shuttle gets from point A to point B, that sort of thing?"

Kenner sensed Andrea's irritation, and her hunch was confirmed when the said, "This isn't the visitor center, Miss Hutchings. We don't have a lot of time for extraneous, non-value-add activities. You need to start looking at the technical…"

Kenner hated it when someone told her what she had to do and, equally maddening, what not to do. Don't say that, don't hold your pencil like that, don't sit there, don't pick a book from that section, don't read ahead, don't ask teachers questions they can't answer, sit down, be quiet, don't say that, sit up straight, and a multitude of other things.

She forced herself to not snap back at her new acquaintance. Obviously Andrea was under a lot of pressure, but that was no excuse to be snotty and opinionated. "I need to see the big picture before I can drill down and figure out what's going on. It helps my overall understanding so I'll be able to put things in better context."

Kenner didn't understand why she added the last statement. She didn't need to explain herself or her work methods to this woman. She had called her to solve their problem.

Andrea looked as if she were about to say something, then thought better of it. Her jaw was clenched when she said, "All right, this way." Andrea pointed in the opposite direction. "We'll start at the beginning.

❖

"So what is your job here, exactly?" Kenner asked as they stepped into a large, cool room. The room had windows on all four sides of the room, giving the occupants a panoramic view of the entire grounds.

Kenner could see dozens of buildings from this vantage point, the largest bearing the blue-and-white NASA logo and an even larger US flag draped down one side.

"Prior to liftoff, the Launch Control Center at the Kennedy Space Station in Florida controls everything. Responsibility for spacecraft remains with them until the booster has cleared the launch tower, when it's handed over to the MCC here in Houston."

"MCC?"

"Mission Control Center," she said. "I have ultimate responsibility for decisions made from that point on. Before the flight it's mainly meetings, training, and paperwork. I lead the team whose responsibility it is to accomplish the objectives of the mission. We also train extensively on the console, so by the time we get to the real thing we're prepared for every contingency."

"So you're the big boss?" Kenner asked. Judging by the look on Andrea's face, she wouldn't have given herself that title.

"The flight director on console is the mission's ultimate authority on the ground, with the final word on any decisions that must be made," Andrea replied calmly, even though the fire in her eyes told a different story.

"So tell me how all this works," Kenner asked, picking up a model of the shuttle from a side table.

"Is this really necessary, Ms. Hutchings? We're wasting time."

Kenner forced herself not to throw it back in this woman's face that it was her time they were intruding on. "I'm a big-picture thinker. I need to get a feel for how it all went together before I can help figure out what might have gone wrong." Kenner didn't see or hear anything, but she could have sworn Andrea said something like "For God's sake."

"The shuttle is over one hundred and eighty feet long and consists of three major components. Most important is the orbiter, which everyone calls the shuttle. It contains the crew and the mission's payload—the items or the equipment they'll be using during the mission. It's fifty-seven feet long and has a wingspan of seventy-eight feet. The large external tank holds fuel for the main engines and the two solid rocket boosters, which provide eighty percent of the launch thrust and most of the shuttle's lift during the first two minutes of flight. The main job of the tank is to hold over five hundred thousand gallons of super-cold liquid hydrogen and liquid oxygen. The two solid rocket boosters on either side provide most of the power to get the shuttle off the ground and out of Earth's orbit. Depending on the mission, the overall weight can range from three million pounds to over eight million. Of course there have been a lot of upgrades and improvements since the first shuttle, including something so simple as saving six hundred pounds by not painting the tank white."

Andrea pointed to each of the components as she referenced them, but Kenner was more interested in her long fingers than the equipment. Trying to regain her focus she asked, "I thought it was called the shuttle."

"Orbiter was the official name for the vehicle. In the early of space flight that's all it did—orbit the Earth, thus the orbiter. The nomenclature hadn't changed throughout the years until recently. The public calls it the shuttle, and we've pretty much adopted the word as well."

Kenner wasn't sure if she detected a slight distaste in Andrea's mouth at her last statement. "Why do you launch from Florida?"

Andrea had that exasperated look again. "For several reasons. First, it's close to the equator, which because of the linear velocity of Earth's surface gives a fuel-saving boost to spacecraft attempting to escape Earth's gravity."

Kenner understood exactly what Andrea was saying. "And the second?"

"The second reason we don't really talk about, and that's because we don't fly over people that might get killed if stuff dropped off or blew up."

"I can understand that's one of those need-to-know items," Kenner said, grimacing. "And the third?"

"Because nothing else is there. When the station was first built, only orange groves grew there. The island has good logistics and the navy base, and an army base is located not too far away."

"Makes sense," Kenner said without much thought.

"I'm so glad you approve," Andrea replied sarcastically. Kenner bit back a comment. She'd have time for that later.

"Tell me about the orbiter, more specifics," Kenner asked, getting to the meat of why she was here.

"The orbiter resembles a conventional aircraft, with double-delta wings swept eighty-one degrees at the inner leading edge and forty-five degrees at the outer leading edge. Its vertical stabilizer's leading edge is swept back at a fifty-degree angle," Andrea said with much more enthusiasm than her previous answers to her other questions. Kenner listened intently to the rest of the details, absorbing everything Andrea was saying.

"I thought it needed booster rockets to lift off. If it landed on the moon, how was it supposed to get back up?"

"We've developed new technologies in the past fifteen years to give the shuttle more thrust per square inch. That and the fact that the gravity on the moon is only seventeen percent of the earth's."

Kenner had no idea how much time had passed, but suddenly she was hungry. "How about some lunch?"

Andrea shot up in surprise. "Ms. Hutchings," she said, obviously exasperated. "Didn't you grasp the gravity of the situation? Seven people are depending on us to bring them home."

Andrea's accent was more pronounced when she was angry. Kenner would file that observation away for future reference. "I know exactly the gravity of the situation," Kenner said calmly. "That's why we're here. So I'll ask you the same questions I asked in the meeting. Are they in any immediate danger?"

"No."

"Are they in any short-term danger?"

"No, but—"

Kenner held both hands up as if to stop the flow of questions. "How long can your crew," she emphasized the word *your* to show Andrea that she understood her sense of responsibility to the crew, "stay up there?"

"If resources are allocated accordingly, anywhere between eight and twelve days."

"Okay, then we have some time to figure it out," Kenner said.

Andrea stepped back and put her hands on her hips. "Let me get this straight. Because we have some time," Andrea intentionally used Kenner's words, "we don't have to start figuring this out right away. And we can, what...go out to lunch?" she said, not trying to disguise her disgust.

She's kind of hot when she gets riled, Kenner thought. There's something interesting behind that calm exterior. "No, Andrea, that's not at all what I'm saying. As a scientist you can appreciate that it's a proven fact that the body, including the brain, needs fuel to gather data, understand it, synthesize it, and know what to do with it. I haven't eaten much the last few days. I was on a plane for God knows how many freaking hours, at your command, by the way, and I'm hungry. So I'm going to get some lunch, and you can either come along and we can talk more about this problem, or you can open your peanut butter and jelly sandwich or whatever you bring for lunch. I'll be back in an hour."

Kenner waited a beat, then shrugged in a way that said "up to you," turned around, and headed to the exit door. When she didn't hear footsteps behind her, she stopped and asked the security officer at the desk the location of the cafeteria. A facility this size had to have one, and even though she was looking forward to eating, she was looking forward to running through the gauntlet of security again even less. Kenner headed out the door and had to keep telling herself not to turn around to see if Andrea was following.

CHAPTER NINE

T-minus 09:11:01:41

"This is fucking unbelievable," Andrea said after Kenner left. Thankfully no one else was in the room to hear her verbalize her frustration. From the minute she'd talked to Kenner on the phone, just thirty-five hours ago, she was aggravated. She supposed it might have something to do with the fact that even though they were a cohesive team, everyone asked "how high" when she said "jump" because she was clearly in charge. However, Ms. Hutchings (Kenner, Andrea corrected herself and agreed with her boss Barry, what the hell kind of name was that) had been insolent the entire time. She'd hardly said a word during the briefing and had asked all of her questions during the site tour. My God, she sounded like a tourist. All she needed was a big hat and a fanny pack, and she'd fit right in. No, Andrea said to herself, no way would she would fit in with any crowd.

Kenner was nothing like Andrea had envisioned her to be. She'd imagined a plump, nerdy woman with thick glasses, bad hair, and unimpressive social skills. Kenner, on the other hand, was almost as tall as she was, thin but curvy in all the right womanly places, had piercing clear green eyes, and was inquisitive. Maybe that was what had thrown her off; Kenner wasn't at all what she'd expected. But wasn't she being hypocritical? She probably wasn't what Kenner had expected either.

However, something about Kenner didn't sit right with Andrea. She wasn't comfortable around her and knocked her off her game. She was on edge and didn't like it. As a result, admittedly, she'd been a little snarky when Kenner invited her to lunch. Actually, she'd probably been downright rude, but damn it, this was a serious situation. Then again, Andrea realized this wasn't Kenner's mission. Kenner wasn't ultimately responsible for the crew. Kenner obviously had more work-life balance, evidenced by the traces of a hickey on the back of her neck.

They were just different, and so many of her colleagues were just like her. They shared a certain NASA red, white, and blue that probably would make someone from the outside looking in think they were all clones. They all dressed the same, thought the same way, and had been educated in the same dozen places. Rarely did they hang out together after hours, and rarely did they chat about personal things during work. From the little she knew of Kenner, she didn't think she would ever fit in a place like this. She would need something more thought-provoking, more exciting. And with her charm and those looks, she probably got everything she was looking for.

Andrea hadn't known Kenner was a lesbian, but the instant she saw her in the conference room this morning she was certain. She'd tried to hide her surprise, but the look in Kenner's eyes had told her she wasn't successful. She doubted any of the other people in the room saw it, and if they did they wouldn't have recognized what it was. A lot of these people had no clue what was going on around them, and none of them knew she was a lesbian too. She never discussed it, didn't talk about her weekends or where she went on vacation, and they never asked. For the first time she felt an uncomfortable sense of hollowness in the center of her chest. Shaking it off as either hunger or fatigue, she exited the observation room and headed to the mission-control room.

❖

The tension in the mission-control room was thick. Working space at each specialist station was crowded with multiple technicians staring at monitors and analyzing data. What Andrea didn't see for the first time, however, was teams talking to each other. She reflected on Kenner's comment about needing to see the entire picture to understand how things related in order to determine the problem and ultimate solution. The teams typically worked well together, and Andrea made a note to bring everyone together when Kenner returned from lunch to discuss their findings so far.

After listening in for a few minutes at each station, she retreated to her desk to prepare the report she needed to send to Barry by the end of the day. When she reached the section about Kenner, she let her hand grow still over the keyboard.

What should she say about the woman who had invaded their neat, orderly world with her brilliant mind yet casual attitude, well-worn jeans and scuffed boots? Andrea knew she was smart and detected traces of her inquisitiveness and her grasp of concepts by the questions she asked. She realized she had been a little harsh when she had considered her little more than a tourist and herself nothing more than a tour guide. Regretfully she realized that her first impression, her second, and her third were probably off the mark.

She never jumped to conclusions like this. Leaping without knowing exactly the speed, trajectory, and angle, and landing zone could get you into serious trouble. Andrea's life was as orderly and planned as the mission she commanded. She left nothing to chance, and she never made a move unless she knew exactly the outcome. Guessing and hoping was never an option, and going with her gut instinct was even less. She was a scientist. Everything had a cause and effect, and Kenner was causing an unease Andrea couldn't shake.

CHAPTER TEN

T-minus 09:10:27:09

"Do you come here often?" Kenner asked the woman in front of her in the checkout line. It was a ridiculous pickup line, but for some reason it always worked for her. If nothing else it was an icebreaker that immediately started conversation. Along with four or five other women in the large cafeteria, the woman was obviously a lesbian but the only one close enough to start a conversation with. The lame question worked, and she turned around and met Kenner's eyes. They were dark brown and held no sense of amusement.

Holding her tray with both hands, Kenner shrugged as much as she could. "Hey, I'm new here," she replied, turning on her charm and turning on her best smile. "Just trying to get the lay of the land, you know. Who's with who, where to sit, coveted spaces, you know, that sort of thing."

The woman eyed her suspiciously. Normally this approach worked, and rarely did she go home alone, but this time she wasn't so sure. Sure, the cafeteria at the Johnson Space Center was the most unusual place she'd ever tried to pick up a woman, but she apparently wasn't going to have any time to cruise any of the local lesbian hangouts. This place was as good as any. Unfortunately, this woman didn't think the same way.

"It's open seating," she said before turning around and stepping forward as the line moved.

Ouch, thought Kenner. She hadn't been rejected like that in… well…ever. "I knew I wasn't going to like this gig," she mumbled. She found an empty table and set her tray on the sturdy, institutional top. The chair squeaked on the floor but nobody seemed to notice, or maybe it was such an everyday occurrence no one bothered to look up from their food. Said chair was hard and uncomfortable, and Kenner knew she wouldn't linger any longer than she had to.

A middle-aged man, with more belly than shirt and shorter legs than his inseam, walked in front of her. He glanced at her, and for a moment Kenner thought he might sit at her table. Lucky for him he kept moving. While she ate, Kenner observed the people in the large room. The area itself was nothing exciting to talk about. Big, square, and full of tables of varying shapes, some large enough to accommodate a dozen, others as few as two. It reminded her of the lunchroom at any number of government buildings she'd been in. Large, industrial, and devoid of any personality or aesthetics to encourage relaxation or conversation. That would have entailed an interior designer willing to tackle such a project, with the government procurement-system hoops to jump through to get there.

The cafeteria was filled with an eclectic group of people ranging in age from the teenage airman sitting with his buddies at a table not far from hers to an elderly man in the checkout line, who, Kenner estimated, was no less than seventy. Hair styles for the men ran the gamut of air-force recruit to dreadlocks. The style of clothing was just as diverse. Everything from shorts and flip-flops to silk ties. Military uniforms of all four branches were also displayed around the room.

She was inquisitive by nature and people her favorite subjects. They never ceased to surprise her—everything from talking with their mouth full to picking their nose while stopped at a red light. Like the windows of the two-thousand-pound vehicle they were driving had one-way glass and the driver could see out but no one could see in.

Kenner didn't see anyone she recognized from the introductions earlier that morning. Maybe they had their own lunchroom behind one of the many closed doors that lined the perimeter of the control room. Maybe Director Finley didn't let them eat. Kenner would bet her next paycheck that she didn't let them eat or drink anything at their workstation. Twenty minutes later she was asking directions to the control room.

The guard at the entrance door was different from the one earlier, and she looked at her badge, then at Kenner, then back at her badge again. The picture was one you'd expect on a standard, unflattering, company security badge. Blue background, camera lens too close, flash too bright, making her natural olive skin look washed out. The guard flipped a few papers on her clipboard, checked her badge again, then Kenner's face before saying, "Thank you," and stepped aside. Kenner didn't even try to make conversation with this lesbian, her don't-fuck-with-me vibe coming through loud and clear. If the woman ever used her handcuffs, it would not involve fun and games.

Kenner stepped through the door into a huge area dominated by an IMAX-sized screen in the front. Along each side of the main screen hung smaller ones, each displaying a different image of what Kenner surmised was the interior of the shuttle, but that was as specific as she could be. It took a few minutes for her eyes to adjust to the low lighting. Five rows of workstations spanned the entire width of the room in a horseshoe arrangement, each on a raised floor, allowing an unblocked view of the screens in front of them. "Wow."

Three or four monitors with digital readouts, trajectory lines, and other monitoring information made up each workstation. A large black plaque with white letters identifying the function rose from the center of each area. Everyone had a headset on or a Bluetooth stuck in their ear, and the chatter of conversations was loud. How did these people think with all this noise and distraction? Her ADD kicked in full throttle. Every man she could see wore a long-sleeve white shirt and tie, and she noticed more than a few bare legs peeking out from under skirts. Red lights flashed above a few of the consoles, green on several more. She forced herself to concentrate on one thing at a time.

The middle screen obviously showed an interior shot of the flight deck of the shuttle, and it looked like cameras must have been placed on the surface of the moon, their lenses facing the shuttle. On the right were a series of digital readouts, but she had no idea what they were telling the dozens of people in the room.

Her visual tour of the room stopped at Andrea. Her station was located in the back of the room, raised on its own separate platform. She sat completely straight in her chair, her hands over a keyboard in perfect ergonomic form. When Kenner was at the keyboard she usually slouched down so low she could barely see over the desk. Kenner watched as Andrea's fingers flew, occasionally pausing as she referenced something on the screen in front of her. She looked like a queen on her throne.

If she thought Andrea was captivating in the meeting this morning, she found Andrea in her element mesmerizing. For lack of a better phrase, her sheer presence exuded confidence and self-assurance. Kenner was enthralled. When Andrea looked her way and saw her, her fingers instantly stopped moving, as if someone had pulled a plug.

A jolt shot through Kenner as if something had been plugged *into* her. Warmth spread down her back, toyed with the idea of settling in the pit of her stomach, but landed in that favorite spot between her legs. Kenner had slept with all types of women, of many nationalities and intellectual levels, but something about Andrea Finley set her apart from any woman that had come before her. Kenner was stunned by her reaction to Andrea, and it wasn't a comfortable feeling.

Trying to shake it off, she walked toward Andrea's console, concentrating on putting one foot in front of the other. She felt giddy, like she was walking across an empty dance floor to ask a girl to dance for the first time. Good God, she thought. What in the hell was going on? Andrea was just a woman, albeit a stunningly beautiful, smart woman, yet a woman nonetheless. And this was work. Even though the lights were low and a hum of tension was definitely in the air, this wasn't a nightclub.

Andrea was surprised to see Kenner standing in her control room watching her. "I didn't expect to see you here," she said.

"Why's that?"

"I didn't think you knew where I was or how to get here." *And that will be the last time I underestimate you,* she added to herself. Kenner smiled and Andrea's heart skipped. *WTF?*

"I asked for directions. Everyone is so helpful. Except for the guard at the door. She's a bit of a grump," Kenner added in a tone that said *if you know what I mean.*

"She's just doing her job," Andrea said and then was angry at herself for defending the guard. She didn't need to explain or justify anyone or anything to Kenner.

"And she does it quite well. She looked at me so thoroughly I thought she could see right down to my skivvies."

Andrea had chosen that moment to take another sip of her cold coffee, and it was all she could do to keep it from spewing out her nose at Kenner's description. As it was, she choked on it and started coughing.

"Are you okay?" Kenner asked, patting her firmly on the back.

Andrea wasn't able to say anything but nodded instead as she tried desperately to take a breath. *Jesus, how embarrassing,* she thought and was finally able to inhale a full breath. She hoped her voice didn't sound as shaky as she felt.

"I'm fine, thanks," she said, clearing her throat. "Must have gone down the wrong pipe," she added. *And almost killed me.*

"I hate it when that happens." Kenner patted her on the back until Andrea realized she was still doing it. "Sorry. You sure you're okay?"

"Yes, I'm fine, thanks. So how was lunch?" *How was lunch? Jesus, Andrea, could you have come up with a more stupid question? First you berate her for going to lunch, and then you ask how it was. Like this is some normal, everyday work conversation. Pull it together.*

"Good, thanks," Kenner replied and pointed to the main screen. "What are they doing?"

Andrea was relieved that the focus had shifted from her making a fool of herself to the mission. Here she was on solid ground. "That's Commander Hight and mission specialist Molly Tremain. We've asked them to limit their movements to conserve the oxygen and food they have left onboard."

"How long have they been up there?"

Did she detect a little bit of awe in Kenner's question? "Nine days, six hours, twenty-four minutes," she said after glancing on the readout above the screen.

"Is everything so exact?" Kenner asked seriously.

"Absolutely. We have very little margin for error." Andrea hoped her voice didn't sound as forceful as it felt. There was no margin for error in space flight. One second too long, one transposed number, one hiccup in a program could spell disaster or worse.

"Did you learn all this at MIT?"

"I beg your pardon?" Andrea had to ask. Kenner had switched the topic so quickly she didn't follow.

"I asked if you learned all this at MIT. I read in your bio that you're a fellow alum."

"Yes, I mean no." Andrea corrected herself, then corrected that response. "No, I didn't learn this at MIT, and yes, I am an alum."

"What did you think of the place?" Kenner asked.

"What place? MIT?"

Kenner nodded.

"It was fine." That was a lame statement, Andrea thought, for describing one of the most prestigious and difficult-to-get-into graduate schools in the world.

"Fine? Did you go to the same school I went to?"

"Okay," Andrea said. "It was tough, challenging, and one of the most difficult things I've ever done." Andrea was surprised that she'd divulged something so personal to a complete stranger.

"Bet you got straight As."

Andrea didn't know if Kenner was complimenting her or mocking her. She was proud of her accomplishments, not only at MIT but in all of her education. It had been a bitch, her entire focus on studying, and she had, in fact, earned all As. She had faced a lot of shit being a woman in courses taught by an all-male faculty and attended by ninety-nine percent men. She had stayed between the lines, and her exacting nature had kept her there.

"I did all right." Andrea answered even though it wasn't a question.

"You must have had Professor Tyrell. She was older than dirt when I was there, but God, she was brilliant. And I swear she had eyes in the back of her head. She saw everything. We didn't get away with anything in her class."

Even though Andrea had had the professor in question for not one but three classes, and she agreed with Kenner's description of the octogenarian, she didn't comment. Instead she said, "This isn't homecoming. We don't have time to reminisce about football games, bonfires, and our college days."

Kenner's eyes narrowed, and she looked at her like she had just stepped on something.

"What?"

"I'm just making conversation about something we have in common. No need to rip my head off, for God's sake."

"We just—"

"I know. Don't have time," Kenner said, shaking her head. "What do you need me to do?"

❖

The digital readout on the screen in front of her read eight fifty-three when Andrea looked up. Jesus, where had the time gone? She looked around the control room and saw that the evening crew was hard at work. The team worked twelve-hour shifts, ensuring continuity in monitoring and status updates. Once the day shift had briefed their relief, Andrea had gathered the outgoing shift together and, along with Kenner, received a complete briefing of their activities.

She looked around the room for Kenner. She was sitting at one of the consoles, pointing to the screen, writing something down and talking to the three men clustered around her. Andrea watched for a few minutes and saw that the men were riveted to what she was saying, each one quickly jotting notes down on paper in front of him.

Kenner was left-handed, and for some stupid reason Andrea thought left-handed women were just plain sexy. She hadn't thought about that in a long time because she was so focused on the mission, the left- or right-handedness of her staff not important. But Kenner wasn't on her staff, and Andrea felt the stirrings of something uncomfortable. She didn't have the time or the interest for this.

Her knee popped as she stood, reminding Andrea she'd been sitting in one position too long. While a midfielder on her lacrosse team in high school, she'd torn her ACL and broken her femur in a nasty collision with a girl half her size. Eighteen agonizing months later she'd given up on the sport and settled down as a freshman at MIT. She flexed her knee several times before putting weight on it and walking toward Kenner.

"So the angle of the pattern of the arc in the data suggests that the trajectory is off only zero point zero, zero two, and that causes the hesitation you see here," Kenner said, her finger tracing a green line on the screen.

Andrea looked over Kenner's shoulder at the screen and quickly scanned the data. It was a bit more complex than she was used to, but it was obvious by the men's reaction that they had learned something new.

One of the men noticed her. "Andrea, Kenner found something we hadn't seen before. We're going to run it through some modeling and simulation to see where it goes," he said with the enthusiasm of someone who'd just discovered the cure for the common cold.

Andrea was impressed, and a glimmer of hope twinkled far in the distance. The other two men turned her way with equal gleeful looks, while Kenner's expression remained neutral.

"Excellent," she said, tired but enthusiastic. "Keep at it, and have Stephanie call me the minute it pans out. I'm headed home." Andrea hated leaving, but she couldn't stay here twenty-four hours a day every day until the crisis was resolved. She wasn't expected to. She had a team of the brightest minds working on this and she had to remain sharp, but to do so she needed to get some sleep. Something she hadn't had much of for the past week.

"I'll think I'll head out too, guys," Kenner said. "You know what to do from here. Keep on that track. You have my cell-phone number. Call me if you run into any trouble. Otherwise I'll see you in the morning."

Kenner stood, placed her hands in the small of her back, and arched backward. Her breasts pushed against her tight shirt, her head fell back, and she let out a low moan. "God, that feels good," she said. Andrea's mouth went dry and her jaw became slack.

"Do you know where I'm staying?" Kenner asked as she started walking away from the workstation. Andrea had to hustle to catch up, her legs refusing to move for a few seconds.

"I think they put you at the Marriott. The details are in my office. It's this way," she said, exiting the control room and turning right. Andrea was suddenly very tired. It was as if the command center was a pressure cooker, the pressure released as soon as she stepped out of the room. But she had to focus for a few more minutes. Kenner followed her to her office.

"I knew it," Kenner said excitedly.

"Excuse me?" Andrea asked, walking over to her desk.

"I read an article about you on the flight and saw a picture of you in an office. I bet myself that it was yours, and bingo, I'm right." Kenner actually pumped her fist in the air.

"What are you talking about?"

"The article about you in *Time* magazine. This is the desk in the picture. And this is the table with these exact models that were to your right." Kenner sounded like a little girl who'd just discovered there really was a Santa.

Andrea hated the article and had wanted nothing to do with the interview until Barry had told her to cooperate. Grudgingly she'd complied, and her sister Beth had bragged that their parents had bought out every issue in their small town of Elk City, Oklahoma.

"You're very observant," Andrea replied, not wanting to have this conversation.

"One of my many good and bad talents," Kenner said almost sadly.

"Why do you say that? Keen observation is very important in what you do." At least she thought so.

"Well, mine can be a bit daunting to some people."

"How so?" Andrea asked, surprisingly interested in Kenner's answer.

"I remember everything, and sometimes it's just a pain in the ass." Kenner frowned.

"Remember everything, like a photographic memory?"

"You know that technically such a trait doesn't exist."

"Yes, I know. But I do believe that some people have the ability to remember things in much more minute detail than others. Almost like a mental snapshot."

"Good, because that's me. I don't want you to think I'm some sort of freak," Kenner said quickly.

Andrea detected something she couldn't put her finger on in Kenner's comment. She had lost her cutting edge, and her flippant attitude wasn't as strong as usual. Too tired to figure out the cause she said, "Let's go. I'll drop you off at your hotel."

CHAPTER ELEVEN

T-minus 09:01:12:17

"What do you mean they don't have your reservation?" Kenner was standing beside her car door. Andrea was still parked in the circle drive of the hotel checking her email when she happened to glance up and see Kenner just about where she'd left her. She motioned her over.

"You heard me, they don't have my reservation."

"Why don't they give you another room? We can figure out the billing tomorrow."

"They don't have any empty rooms, and the desk clerk said there's not one within thirty miles. Because of the mission and the Comic Con convention and the Harley Davidson annual showcase in town, everything's booked."

"I don't care if the circus is in town. You need a room" Andrea was furious, which was completely out of character for her. But the strain of the past few weeks and the arrival of Kenner Hutchings had thrown her off kilter. And now there wasn't a single hotel room in the area? "Don't hotels have empty rooms they give out in situations like this?"

"How in the hell do I know?" Kenner answered abruptly. "Don't you NASA types check and double-check everything three times?"

"Of course we do," Andrea shot back. "Never mind," she said, too exhausted to continue this absurd conversation. She unlocked the car's doors and indicated the passenger seat with her thumb. "Get in."

"What?"

"I said get in. I'm too tired to drive all over town trying to find you another place."

Kenner hesitated, and Andrea's already missing patience completely disappeared.

"Are you going to get in the car?" She actually wanted to say, "Get your ass in the car or sleep in the street. I don't care," but even in her pissed-off state, she knew she couldn't do that. Barry would do more than just read her the riot act; he might even remove her from the mission. Such a response would be career suicide. "Kenner, just get in," she said instead.

Kenner hesitated a few more moments as if deciding if it was better for her to go with Andrea or take her chances on the street to find her own hotel. Finally, just before Andrea blew a gasket, Kenner walked around in front of her car and climbed in. She tossed her duffle bag on the seat behind them.

"You know you're kinda cute when you get mad. Your eyes flash, and the tips of your ears get red."

Andrea was speechless. Had Kenner just hit on her? It had been a long time and absolutely never at work, but really? Did this woman always have an attitude like this? How was Andrea supposed to work with her? This was a life-threatening situation, and if Kenner wasn't going to take this seriously…Andrea hoped she wouldn't have to figure that out.

Kenner looked at her expectantly. What was she supposed to say to that? Don't say anything like that again? That borders on sexual harassment? Thank you? To keep this day from getting worse she simply said, "Buckle your seat belt."

❖

"Where are we?" Kenner asked. It was dark, but she could tell this was a residential area, not a commercial one.

"My house." Andrea's reply was clipped.

Andrea hadn't said a word on the drive, and Kenner was smart enough not to try to make conversation. It was obvious Andrea had a plan, and in no way was Kenner going to question it. She was smarter than to ask for trouble.

"Your house?"

"Yes. I have a guest room that rarely gets used, with clean sheets on the bed and fresh towels in the bathroom. You have to sleep somewhere, and I'm too exhausted to try to find you anything else." Andrea pulled into the drive, pushed a button on the visor, and the garage door slowly started to slide open.

"You don't have to do this. I can find something." Kenner knew it was a little late for such a comment, but she had to say something. Her mother had taught her as much.

"Too late, we're already here," Andrea replied briskly.

Andrea's house was a modest brick two-story that looked similar to, yet different from the others on the street. Judging by the architecture and the size of the trees in the front yard, the neighborhood must have been built several decades ago, when pride in craftsmanship overruled cookie-cutter sub-divisions. A circular drive led to the garage, which was tucked discreetly at the side of the house.

Kenner had never desired to be a homeowner. Being one would cement her feet in commitment, and she didn't do commitment. It meant keeping the yard neat and tidy, making sure the trash got carried out to the street on garbage day, and paying the water bill. All that was too much responsibility for her taste, and she was definitely not the white-picket-fence kind of girl.

Kenner wasn't surprised when she saw the contents of Andrea's garage as the door rose. Everything was in its place. There were no shelves, but on one side sat a large work bench with tools hanging in perfect order on a pegboard attached to the wall. A bright-red shiny toolbox sat adjacent to the workbench, and

Kenner suspected if she looked closely she could see her reflection in the top. A name-brand road bike was suspended from the ceiling by a set of cables and pulleys, a sparkling clean John Deere lawn tractor parked below it. Kenner didn't have a garage but reflected on the contents of her apartment, and compared to this she could be a candidate for the TV reality show *Hoarders*.

She grabbed her bag out of the backseat and followed Andrea into the house. A series of beeps later the alarm was disabled and the lights turned on. Andrea tossed her keys on a side table and walked farther into the room.

They entered the house through the amazingly large kitchen. The island had to be at least eight feet long and five or six feet wide. The granite countertops gleamed under the can lights from the ceiling high overhead. There were more cabinets than Kenner could count at first glance, the appliances stainless and all high-end. Very impressive, and not what she would have expected from the serious, all-business flight director. She said as much.

"Not that it's any of your business what I do in my spare time, but I like to cook."

"With this kitchen, the phrase 'I like to cook' is like saying 'I like to fly' as you're catapulted off the flight deck of an aircraft carrier."

Andrea didn't say anything, just led the way to a room to the right of a large entertainment center. "The guest room is over here." She switched on the light. "The bathroom's through there." She pointed. "Make yourself at home. Are you hungry? I'm not sure what's in the fridge. I've been a little busy lately," she said sarcastically, her accent a little more pronounced.

Kenner had had enough of Andrea's snarky attitude. She blocked Andrea from leaving. "Look, I didn't ask to come here. You brought me here before I even had a chance to say no thanks." Kenner pointed at Andrea to emphasize her point. "You're obviously from somewhere in the South, and I know your mama taught you better manners than the way you've treated me since I got here to solve *your* problem. If you don't want me to stay, just say the word, because I can get on the next plane as fast as I got on the last one. And have a hell of a lot more fun when I get *there*."

It was a face-off, and Kenner would be damned if she'd give in first. She was here as a favor to NASA and didn't want or expect special treatment, but she wouldn't let this woman or anyone else on this rocket ship shit on her.

Andrea didn't move and seemed to be deciding if she would say anything. "I'm just tired," she said, expelling a frustrated sigh. "It's not an imposition to have you here. Please make yourself at home. My room is down the hall, last door on the left, if you need anything. Good night."

Were her words rushed? Kenner wondered. Was she in a hurry to get out of this small room as much as Kenner wanted her to? Was it for the same reason? She doubted it. With a woman like Andrea, she probably thought the sooner to bed the sooner she could go back to work. And that was really sad.

Kenner knocked on the bedroom door. "Andrea?" When she didn't get an answer, she knocked a little louder. She couldn't be asleep. It was only five minutes since Andrea had left her room. "Andrea? A dog's barking and scratching at the back door. He definitely wants to come in. It is yours?" When Andrea still didn't answer, Kenner turned the knob and opened the door a few inches.

"Andrea?" she called, not sure if she should go in or just go to bed and put a pillow over her head. The bed was still made, and Kenner took a quick glance around the room. It was large, she guessed at least twenty by thirty. A set of bay windows with white plantation shutters filled one entire side. They were open slightly, letting the light of the full moon splinter into the room.

"Andrea?" she said again, taking a few more steps into the bedroom. She didn't want to startle her, but if she was...*Oh my God.* From where Kenner stopped she could see Andrea's reflection in a large mirror. She was buck-ass naked except for the soap sliding down her back. But that didn't really count because more skin was showing than soap covering it.

Holy Toledo, Kenner thought as her eyes quickly moved over Andrea's wet body. Kenner's hands began to tingle. Andrea was too thin but still had all the right curves in all the right places. Her ass was perfect, and Kenner opened and closed her fists as if she were squeezing each cheek. She licked her lips and swallowed as she focused on the way Andrea's hands slid up and down her body. If Kenner didn't know better she would have thought Andrea was putting on a show for her. And she had the front-row seat.

Andrea washed one arm, then the other, soaping her breasts and stomach in between. Kenner raised her eyebrows as if somehow she could encourage her hands to drift lower and disappear between her legs. Kenner loved to watch a woman pleasure herself, but she wasn't sure she could stand on the sidelines and watch. Not this time. Kenner's legs felt weak when Andrea lifted one of her legs and placed her foot on the seat in the corner. When she bent over to wash her calf, Kenner stifled a gasp of pleasure and quickly took a step backward.

"Kenner?"

She froze. Andrea had obviously heard her or she sensed Kenner's presence. Should she come clean and confess her voyeurism and offer to wash her back? The other alternative was to say something and pretend she'd just come in. Or she could simply slink out the same way she came in and take her vision of Andrea's naked body to bed with her. She opted for the last choice, backed out of the room, and silently closed the door she'd opened a few minutes earlier.

Kenner's legs shook as she hustled back down the hall to her own room. She shut the door and leaned against it, her heart hammering. She was breathing fast and felt like she'd just run several miles at top speed. Her hands trembled as she scrubbed them over her face in an attempt to calm down.

Good God, it wasn't like she was a teenager and had caught the mother of one of her friends in the shower. She was a grown-up woman, and Andrea definitely was as well. The scene from *The Graduate* flashed in her mind just before she heard a knock on her door. She jumped and dashed over and hopped into the bed, pulling the covers up over her. She usually slept nude but hadn't had a chance to take her clothes off because of the barking dog. Which, by the way, she noticed was no longer barking.

"Kenner?" She was startled by Andrea's voice at her door.

"Yeah, come on in."

Andrea opened the door and stuck her head in. Her hair was wet, and even from this distance she smelled fresh and clean.

"I thought I heard something. Everything okay?"

Not hardly. "Yes, everything's fine." *Liar.*

Andrea leaned into the room a little farther, causing the gap in her robe to become even larger, exposing almost all of one breast. "Do you need anything?"

"No, not a thing, thanks." *Big fat liar.* "Good night. I'll see you in the morning, and thanks again," she managed to croak out, needing Andrea and her tempting bare breast to get out of her room.

Kenner tossed the covers off and started fanning herself the instant after she heard the door latch click shut. That was close. The last thing she needed was for Andrea to suspect she'd caught her in the shower. They had enough animosity between them; she didn't need any more. And what was up with that? Sure, Andrea had sounded a little tense when she'd called and asked for her help. Who wouldn't be in her shoes? But what had she done to warrant the antagonism Andrea was heaping on her?

Yet that wasn't what had Kenner all worked up. It was the image of the water sliding off Andrea's naked body. What in the hell was she going to do with that visual? She couldn't un-see it if she wanted to. As Kenner closed her eyes, she knew she didn't.

CHAPTER TWELVE

T-minus 08:17:42:16

Andrea turned off her alarm and fell back onto the bed, exhausted. She hadn't slept much, worrying about the mission, the bills that needed to be paid, that she hadn't called her parents in weeks, and that she probably needed to buy milk. She rolled over and threw her arm over her eyes. Yeah, that and the fact that Kenner Hutchings was in a bed fifteen feet down the hall.

She rolled over onto the back and said to herself, "What in the hell were you thinking bringing her here? You never do anything that stupid. God, I need to have my head examined." In the span of fifteen hours Kenner had come in and thrown her entire life into turmoil. She was trespassing on her well-manicured professional turf, and Andrea had to spend whatever free time she had spelling out acronyms and entering display commands. If her sister knew she'd invited her to stay the night she'd never hear the end of it.

Why were some women like a cool summer shower and others like an F5 tornado? Andrea preferred women that were calm, never got rattled, had miles of patience, and avoided conflict. It just made them that much easier to have around. Everyone knew how to act and what to expect, which was definitely no drama. If she wanted drama she'd be a thespian instead of a lesbian. Pushing thoughts of Kenner out of her head, she started to get up and stopped. What the hell was that smell? She quickly sat up. Coffee?

"Andrea?" Kenner called from the other side of her bedroom door. "Andrea, I heard your alarm. I'm assuming you're up. I brought coffee." She knocked again. "Andrea?"

"Yes, I'm up," Andrea said, trying to get her bearings. She couldn't remember the last time she woke up with someone in her house in the morning. Actually she couldn't remember the last time anyone woke her up for any reason. Jesus, where had that come from?

"May I come in?"

Andrea frantically looked around her room. It was in its usual tidy condition, except for her clothes that lay in a pile on the bathroom floor where she'd left them. She ran her hands through her hair several times. "Sure." Her voice was raspy from sleep, or the lack thereof, and she cleared her throat as the door opened.

Kenner was carrying a mug of coffee, the steam billowing up from the top. It was her favorite mug, white with the logo from John Deere, a yellow deer jumping over a green background. She always used it on the morning she mowed her yard. It was just one of her quirky things absolutely no one knew about.

"Good morning," Kenner said, approaching the bed. Her hair was wet, and she was wearing a pair of low-rise black jeans, a white button-down shirt, and boots. She looked good. She handed Andrea the cup. "Sleep well?"

No. "Yes, you?"

"Pretty good, actually, considering my mind was racing from everything I saw today. I usually have trouble falling asleep." Kenner looked around the room.

Andrea followed Kenner's eyes, trying to see the room as Kenner would. The walls were painted a rich shade of purple accented by white crown molding along the ceiling. Four-inch trim around the closet doors and windows, along with the white shutters, contrasted perfectly with the dark walls. The carpet was tan and thick, the paintings on the walls adding dimension and additional color. When she'd remodeled several years ago, this was the only room the decorator hadn't designed. It was her bedroom, her sanctuary, and she wanted it to reflect her personality. The fact that no one other than Kenner had seen it was depressing. Kenner's gaze finished sweeping the room and came back to her.

"This room is beautiful."

Andrea's stomach did more than flutter, and her pulse raced. Suddenly she felt very self-conscious sitting in her bed in nothing much more than a T-shirt. She fought the urge to pull the covers up higher on her chest because that would just be ridiculous. Kenner's eyes were piercing, as if she could see right through the sheet, blanket, and her T-shirt. Her nipples hardened.

Heat ran through Andrea from the top of her head to the bottom of her feet. Now she wanted to toss off the covers and everything underneath. "Is that for me?" Her voice quivered a bit. Did that question have a double meaning?

Kenner held her gaze as she walked across the room "Yes, black, I hope."

Andrea took the cup from Kenner, trying not to touch any part of Kenner's hand in the process. "Yes, thanks. How did you know?" Andrea blew on the hot liquid and took a tentative sip.

"Process of deductive reasoning. I didn't see any creamer in your fridge or milk, for that matter, and I couldn't find the sugar. They taught us that in grad school," Kenner added, smiling.

Andrea almost choked on her coffee. Kenner's smile was cute and playful. She lit up the room. "Obviously you aced that section," Andrea added, not sure where her sense of humor had come from. She was usually not fit to speak to until after at least two cups of coffee and a hot shower.

Kenner gave her the thumbs-up sign. "A-plus, but I failed miserably in sleeping-in," she added dryly. "I hope you don't mind me scrounging around in your kitchen?"

Andrea took another sip. It was the same coffee grounds, pot, and water as when she made it, but this morning it was delicious. "No, not at all. Especially if it's coffee." She glanced at the clock. "I'll be ready in ten minutes," she said, sliding her legs out and onto the floor.

"No hurry," Kenner was able to say. Actually she was surprised she was able to say anything when Andrea's legs slipped out from the covers. She caught more than a glimpse of a thigh before Andrea's nightshirt fell down and covered it. Kenner knew she should leave, but she couldn't help but stare at Andrea's backside as she walked toward the bathroom. When Andrea turned around, Kenner knew she'd been caught looking. She felt her face flush.

"What are you doing?" Andrea snapped. Before Kenner had a chance to answer, Andrea continued. "Just because I let you stay here last night does not give you the right to ogle me this morning. Now if you'll excuse me." Andrea held her hand palm up, signaling for Kenner to leave the room.

"Hey," Kenner snapped back. "Just a natural reaction. You showed, I looked."

"I didn't *show* you anything," Andrea said, her temper obviously flaring.

"That's not what I saw from over here," Kenner said with a smirk.

"Get out."

She couldn't deny Andrea's anger this time. Kenner boldly took one last look at Andrea's bare legs and left.

WTF, Kenner thought as she walked back to the kitchen. She'd been caught looking like it was the first time she'd seen a half-naked woman. On the contrary, she'd seen more naked women than she could count, and none of them, including her first, had caused her to be as mesmerized as she'd been with Andrea. And her reaction. "Holy Christ," Kenner said back in the kitchen. "She acted like I committed a mortal sin." She needed to solve this work problem and get out of here and back to her vacation, fast.

❖

The tension inside the car was suffocating. Kenner glanced at Andrea several times, noting that her white-knuckled hands strangling the steering wheel were in the correct ten-and-two position. Her jaw muscles were working overtime clenching and unclenching as the miles came and went. Andrea's one- or two-word responses shut down Kenner's attempt to make conversation so she gave it one last shot.

"Is there a problem here?"

"No," Andrea replied, though the tightening of her lips said otherwise.

"What did I do to you? You've been treating me like a piranha ever since I got here. Is it me personally or the fact that you don't want someone intruding on your little island?"

That got Andrea's attention. Her head snapped to the side to look at Kenner, then back at the road just as quickly.

"It is not my little island," she said with barely restrained anger. "And there is nothing wrong."

"Bullshit." Andrea didn't answer. "Did you hear me? I said bullshit. If you treat everyone on this team the way you're treating me, I'm surprised you even have a team."

"Really?" Andrea asked skeptically. "And just how do you think I'm treating you?"

"Like shit," Kenner barked, not even trying to control her anger anymore. "I don't expect you to roll out the red carpet for me, but I do expect you to treat me with professional respect."

"So you expect me to what?" Andrea said, still not looking at her. "Treat you like some prima donna, some Albert Einstein who's going to ride in on your white horse and save the day?"

"First of all, I am not a prima donna. I'm a working stiff, just like everyone else. Second, my IQ is higher than Al's, and I don't have a white horse. I have a blue Harley."

"Hmph." Andrea shook her head in obvious disgust.

"And what does that mean?'

"Nothing."

"Bullshit."

"You know you're beginning to sound like a broken record,"

"Ditto," Kenner replied. "You keep spewing bullshit. And as soon as you stop, I'll stop."

"You sound like a child."

"So now I'm a child?" Kenner replied, incredulous.

"You're what, twenty-four?"

"Twenty-six, and because I happen to be the youngest one in that control room by a decade, and younger than you, that makes me a child?"

"I didn't say you were a child. I said you sounded like a child." Andrea looked left, then right before proceeding into the intersection.

"So now we're going to get into semantics. Well, let me tell you something, Flight Director Finley. I can go toe-to-toe with you all day. I can think of bigger words than you, and I can solve your fucking problem."

At her final statement Andrea turned her head and looked at Kenner. "Why didn't you say so?"

"I didn't say I *did* solve your problem. I said I *can* solve your problem," Kenner stated with a look that said two could play at this game. "I don't expect you to treat me any differently than any other member of this mission crew. And that is with respect. If you don't, I don't care if a hundred lives are depending on me. I'll take my brilliant brain and leave."

"The president of the United States receives a daily update on the status of this issue," Andrea said casually, but her meaning was clear.

"I don't care if the king of the world receives a daily update on the status of this issue," Kenner shot back, mimicking Andrea's words.

They drove the rest of the way in silence. The guard at the main gate glanced at Andrea's badge but scrutinized Kenner's. Obviously her face wasn't nearly as familiar as Andrea's, and he gave her badge a thorough second and third look. They parked in the middle of the parking lot, and as Andrea gathered her briefcase from the backseat, Kenner did the same with her backpack.

"You don't have a reserved parking spot?"

"No."

"Isn't that unusual? Aren't you kind of in charge here?"

Andrea didn't even try to mask her sigh. "No, I'm not in charge. I'm just like anyone else on this mission."

"No, Andrea, you're not just like anybody else on this mission." Kenner mimicked her words. "Do you actually believe that?" The glare in Andrea's eyes warned Kenner of the response to come.

"Yes, I do. I have a responsibility to this mission and to those seven astronauts. I'm no different than Frank, who sits in the chair at communication, or Cynthia, the med tech, or Ron in propulsion. We all have jobs and responsibilities, and mine is no different from anyone else's."

Kenner put her hands up to stop the verbal blows. "Whoa there, Andi. No need to jump down my throat on this. It was just a question."

Andrea stopped so suddenly, it took Kenner several steps before she realized she was no longer beside her. Andrea stepped forward and closed the gap between them.

"Don't *ever* call me that. My name is Andrea," she said through clenched teeth. "And if you can't remember that, then Director Finley will do."

Whoa, Kenner thought. Hit a hot spot, did I? Another interesting sign of emotion. *She does have some fire inside.* Kenner followed Andrea into the security screening area.

By the time they got through security, Kenner's jaws ached from clenching them to keep from saying anything else. Andrea didn't speak to her as she walked into her office and closed the door.

"Well," Kenner said to the plain brown door. "Now who's being childish?"

❖

"God damn it. Why do I let her get to me?" Andrea said, tossing her briefcase onto her desk. The stapler slid across the wooden top and clattered to the floor. That made her angrier because she never allowed herself to lose her temper. "Fuck." She retrieved the stapler and set it in its customary place. Then she sat down and turned on her computer.

While she completed the familiar log-in steps on the computer screen in front of her, she tried to focus and get her head back where it needed to be—in this mission—not on the dark-haired woman who had turned her well-choreographed life upside down.

What was it about Kenner that got under her skin so much? Over the course of her career she'd worked with all kinds of people, with equally varying personality and work styles. Why would working with Kenner be any different? She shook her head and forced herself to concentrate on the information on the screen.

The log of activity and status of every system since she left last night was accounted for. She read through her report quickly, then re-read it carefully, focusing on the notations of the assistant flight director on duty, as well as the reports from each of the mission specialists. With the exception of the fact that the engines wouldn't fire, everything appeared to be business as usual. The crew had slept well and had risen on time, waking to Lady Gaga's song "Born This Way."

She tried to focus on the rest of the evening reports, but her mind kept drifting back to Kenner standing in her bedroom offering her a cup of coffee. She didn't like the way that had made her feel. She was more than a little surprised at the way her body had reacted. She hadn't felt like that in the presence of a woman in, what…Andrea couldn't remember how long. She was definitely out of practice with having a woman in her house, especially in her bedroom, but this was a simple, friendly gesture from a houseguest. Then why had it made her feel so uncomfortable? And when she'd caught Kenner looking at her legs she'd completely overreacted. Jesus, she'd jumped down her throat like she'd kissed her in the middle of the control room. Wouldn't that be something? And the way Kenner had looked when Andrea came out of her bedroom to leave was almost staggering.

Kenner had been dressed in faded 501 button-fly jeans that fit her long legs perfectly, and they'd looked so comfortable and soft, it was all she could do not to cross the room and touch them. Kenner's boots might have been brown at one time, but they too were worn. However, her long-sleeve shirt was blistering white and amazingly not very wrinkled. Her hair was damp from her shower. Thankfully she'd had her back to the room when Andrea walked in, or it would have been her turn to be caught ogling.

Andrea turned her chair away from the monitor and gazed out the window. She liked the familiar, the process, the routine, and whenever she struggled with something regarding the mission, this view settled her. She relished the knowledge that every building was constructed with precision, every activity within its walls and on the entire site completed with perfection. There was no room for error, and that relentless structure suited her perfectly.

A white pickup truck with a wide blue stripe and a flashing blue light on the cab was pulling an open trailer filled with boxes. Even from this vantage point Andrea saw that the boxes were strapped down securely. The driver drove exactly between the lines as he crisscrossed over the area. Whereas others would have cut a corner short or taken a shortcut, this driver stayed exactly between the lines. Andrea reflected a minute and couldn't remember when she'd ever dared to drift outside the lines. Until Kenner Hutchings had walked into her mission.

Andrea frowned as she thought about the way she'd reacted to Kenner. For God's sake, they'd been together less than twenty-four hours, and all they'd done was bicker and trade verbal spars. Kenner was right; she hadn't done anything to deserve such treatment. But something about her unnerved Andrea. Her intelligence didn't threaten her. Far from it. Intelligent women were sexy, left-handed intelligent women even more so, and Kenner was both. But this was business, and not only was she working, but she had a serious situation on her hands. This was not the time to entertain any thoughts that didn't pertain to solving their problem.

Andrea had never been attracted to anyone she worked with. Her single-mindedness didn't allow her to think about anything other than the job in front of her. An ex-girlfriend's parting shot out the door had been that Andrea was nothing more than a clone of one of the many systems that NASA employed to keep their astronauts alive. Andrea hadn't given any thought to the comment at the time, chalking it up to a nasty-breakup low blow. She had feelings, she had emotions. Sure, she wasn't as carefree, as light and airy as someone like Kenner. But she wasn't a machine either.

She'd always been a little on the reserved side, cautious, a thinker first and then a doer. She was happy with her life. She'd reached the pinnacle of her career. Just about everything had worked out according to plan. She'd had a slight detour here and there, but each one had only given her more experience and exposure to do the job she held today. And speaking of the job, she started reading the reports on the screen in front of her out loud. She really needed to focus, and the sound of saying the words aloud made her concentrate on them, plus hearing them reinforced the material. She hadn't had to employ this technique in years, and to do so now, with something so critical in front of her, was unsettling.

"Get back on track, Andrea," she said to herself, looking at the colorful graphic on the screen. Then she picked up a pen and began jotting down a few notes.

❖

Kenner entered the control room, a cup of hot coffee in one hand, a tablet of paper and her favorite pen in the other. The same guard was at the door and repeated the same security checks in exactly the same order as she had yesterday. No one looked up when she entered, and she slowly made her way around the room. She stopped at each station, spending a few minutes reviewing the data displayed and listening to any conversation. These steps gave her a feel for the overall status of that area. Admittedly at some stops she didn't understand anything, but at others she was able to get the general gist of what was going on. All of the information was critical to her understanding of the entire situation.

Kenner had an uncanny ability to see the big picture of a situation and then drill down to the exact cause, issue, or problem and find the solution. The downside was that she couldn't just focus on the problem area. Her mind grasped for reasoning and context and how all things fit together.

Growing up, her thought process had frustrated her parents and just about every teacher she'd had. She was an inquisitive child, and growing up in the small town of Carltown, Arkansas she had been quickly labeled a disruptive student. Carltown, population thirty-eight thousand, four hundred and twelve, was located in the southeast corner of the state, abutting Louisiana and Mississippi. When her teachers were trying to focus on teaching the fundamentals, Kenner was struggling to understand how they all fit together. When the rest of the class was learning the proper sound of the letters A, B, and C, Kenner was lost because she couldn't figure out what that had to do with words, or anything, for that matter. Once she saw how each letter and sound fit into a word, which then fit into a sentence, she excelled in reading. That was just how her brain worked. Unfortunately, the public school system in Carltown wasn't equipped for a student like her, and Kenner suffered because of their inadequacy.

She was brilliant, and living in rural Arkansas and kids being the cruel little shits they can be, they teased and tormented her for being a nerd and a brainiac. She graduated from college at nineteen, finished her master's degree in mathematics at twenty, and her doctorate two years later. As a result she was always the odd-man out, so to speak. The awkwardness wasn't quite as intense in college and as she'd worked on her PhD, but years of being under the microscope both for good and bad reasons had shaped who she was today. Her carefree attitude was more than a front to ward off insensitive, hurtful, jealous comments. It was how she lived her life. She took her work very seriously, having finally found a place to fit in at Quantum, but other than that she was just what she appeared to be. She didn't care what people thought of her, but she agonized over her work at times to a state of complete exhaustion. She drove fast, played hard, and liked her women the same.

A movement of color passed across her peripheral vision, and Kenner turned her head to find it. The royal blue in Andrea's shirt was the first thing she'd noticed this morning when she turned around to see Andrea standing in her living room, staring at her. The second was the way the color made Andrea's eyes stand out, and the third was the way her pulse started racing faster through her body.

Andrea was dressed in a simple black suit, the crease in her pants pressed like a razor, the cuffs draping perfectly over her shoes. She wore a thin black belt around her waist, and had tucked her shirt in perfectly. She seemed to have stopped midway putting her jacket on, one arm in one out, as she stared at Kenner.

"What?" Kenner had asked. But what she had really thought was *what now*?

Andrea had recovered and finished putting on her jacket, her eyes looking everyplace other than at Kenner. "Nothing. Ready? We can grab something for breakfast on the way."

"I didn't see anything in the fridge," Kenner said without thinking. The look on Andrea's face was one she recognized, and she quickly said, in a joking tone, "Yeah, I know. You've been a little busy lately." Andrea had scowled, obviously not finding the humor in her words, and now when she looked at Kenner across the control room she still wasn't smiling.

"Boss wake up on the wrong side of the bed?" Kenner asked the man sitting next to her in the conference room she'd been in yesterday. They'd gathered for the post-shift meeting, and Andrea was again at the head of the table practically barking orders and questioning every status report that was given. The man stifled a laugh, but not well enough.

"Maxwell? Kenner? Is there something you want to share with the team?" Andrea asked expectantly.

Andrea was more than a little cute when she frowned, but Kenner kept her opinion to herself.

"No," the man beside her answered, not looking at Kenner. Andrea's eyes moved to Kenner. She raised her eyebrows as if to say "well"?

"No, ma'am," Kenner replied, the fire in Andrea's eyes telling her she didn't like her answer. "I was just asking Max what the telemetry readings were overnight."

Kenner kept her expression neutral as Andrea searched her face for any sign of deceit.

"And what were they?" she asked, obviously hoping to catch them in a lie.

"Twelve point eight," Kenner answered.

Max let out a sigh of relief.

Andrea stared at her a few seconds more before turning her attention and next question to a small Hispanic woman Kenner hadn't met.

Ten minutes later Kenner couldn't wait to get out of the meeting. She hated meetings and would rather be out solving the problem than talking about it. She put her hands on her thighs to stop her legs from fidgeting, but her feet took up the cadence instead. Finally after what felt like forever, Andrea dismissed them. All except her.

"Kenner?"

Shit, what did she want now? Was it to scold her to dress more professionally? Not to talk in class? Maybe it was that her services were no longer needed. She couldn't care less about the first, would defend herself against the second, and, by the status reports, knew the third wasn't true. She held her ground, braced for God knew what.

"My boss, Barry Haven, wants to see you this morning."

Kenner couldn't help but show her surprise. "Your boss?"

"Yes. His office is this way," Andrea replied, holding her hand out in the direction of one of the doors.

Kenner walked slightly behind Andrea through the crowded halls. One by one the other people turned either left or right down other long halls, and she moved beside her. "How long did it take you to learn your way around this maze?" Kenner asked, her boot heels tapping quietly on the tile floor.

"Three days," Andrea replied seriously, nodding to a man in a flight suit walking in the opposite direction.

"Three days?" Kenner was impressed. She doubted that most people could find their way around in three months. Andrea didn't say any more, probably still pissed about their conversation in the car. Well, too bad. No way was she going to let her or anyone in this place walk all over her. She wasn't changing her modus operandi for anyone.

Finally, after the fifth turn, Andrea stopped in front of a door with a brass nameplate that read Barry Haven. She knocked, opened the door, and stepped inside. A woman who sat behind a large desk raised her hand, signaling to her ear in the proverbial "I'm on the phone" gesture. Since the advent of Bluetooth, you never knew if someone was talking to you, someone else, or to themselves. She finished the call and touched her ear.

"Andrea, good to see you. He's waiting. Would either of you like some coffee?" she asked politely.

"No." Andrea replied at the same time Kenner said "Yes." The woman looked at Andrea, unsure which answer to respond to. "I'd love some, black, if it's not too much trouble," Kenner said. Damn it, she wanted coffee, and when offered she'd take it. She saw Andrea nod slightly before she opened the door to her boss's office.

This office was three times the size of Andrea's and definitely furnished from a different account than hers. Cherrywood furniture gleamed, the carpet was plush, and this was obviously the corner office. A man in his late fifties rose from behind the massive desk.

Kenner held back a laugh when he stood. He couldn't have been more than five feet five inches tall, and now she understood his furnishings. He didn't come out from around his desk to greet them but extended his arm instead. Kenner stepped farther into the room and stopped in front of his desk, the width of it making her lean over to shake his offered hand.

"Ms. Hutchings, thank you for coming," he said in a gravelly voice before sitting back down and motioning to them to do the same. His feet must have been dangling off his chair, because seated behind the desk he looked like he was at least six feet tall.

"I won't say it's my pleasure, but I'm here," she replied, trying to get comfortable in the rock-hard chair.

Her response obviously surprised him, and he looked at Andrea. "She was on vacation when I called and was kind enough to cut it short."

"Yes, that's right," Kenner added. "I was in the south of France on a beach with a cold drink and a hot—"

"She's getting settled in," Andrea said. "She spent most of the day yesterday with Propulsion analyzing data."

Interesting, Kenner thought. Was Andrea afraid of how she might finish her sentence? Barry eyed her critically, taking in everything from her boots to the spike in her hair. Too bad he couldn't see the tattoo on her left forearm. Judging by the look he was giving her, that would send him over the edge.

"Paul and Fred are very sharp," Kenner added, thinking everyone on this crew needed a compliment with this guy. "And Andrea is bending over backward to make me feel welcome."

"As she should. The success or failure," and he emphasized the word failure, "of this mission lies directly on her shoulders."

God, what an ass, Kenner thought. No wonder Andrea was wound tighter than a guitar string. She glanced over at Andrea, who had suddenly turned very pale.

"Her crew will do anything for her, and they're working their damnedest to get the mission back on track." Kenner could sling the political bullshit with the best of them. She hated it, preferring to call it what it was, but she could do it, and this seemed to be the time. She felt Andrea's eyes on her.

"I don't need to tell you this, Mr. Haven, but you have an extremely qualified group on the floor. I've talked to all of them, and kudos to you for getting them. They are some of the brightest minds in the world." Kenner loved to study body language, and as much as Haven thought he was hiding it, he'd gobbled up her compliment completely. He was practically beaming. Then he shifted.

"Then why are *you* here?"

"For the same reason colleagues talk to each other every day. It helps to bounce ideas around, gets the creative juices flowing. The old saying two heads are better than one is true. Except in this case it's more like forty-eight." Good God, it was getting deep in here. She had to leave soon or she'd gag.

"Speaking of getting the mission on track again," Kenner said, rising from her chair, "I need to get back to the control room. It was a pleasure to meet you, Mr. Haven, and thanks for asking me to join your team for a while." Kenner turned to look at Andrea's shocked expression. "If you two have other things to talk about, I can find my way back."

Barry answered for Andrea. "No, that's all." He was obviously trying to regain control of his meeting.

The door had barely closed before Kenner said, "What an asshole." She turned left and started walking down the hall. "And you work for that guy?" she asked Andrea, who had to hurry to keep up with her.

"He's very good at what he does."

"Yeah, at being a pompous ass. What's with him saying 'The success or failure of this mission lies directly on her shoulders,'" she asked, mimicking his nasal voice. "Obviously as the head of NASA the buck doesn't stop with him. And speaking of bucks, how much of my taxpayer dollars went to decorating that office?" Kenner knew that whatever was in her head was coming out of her mouth with very little censorship. "What a jerk, and I'd appreciate it if you keep him away from me because I'm not going to take shit from him either."

Andrea wasn't expecting it when Kenner stopped in front of her and turned around so suddenly she almost ran over her. Kenner's face was flushed and anger sparked in her eyes.

"What is with everyone around here? From the guard at the gate to mister shit head," Kenner said, pointing back down the hall. "Is it a requirement to have a stick up your butt to work here? If it is, no thank you."

Andrea reached out and grabbed Kenner's arm before she could walk away. "We're all under a lot of pressure," she said, her explanation weak.

"And you don't deal with it well. Isn't that something you're screened on—how to handle pressure and stress? If not, it should be, because with a few exceptions all of you suck at it."

"That's not fair," Andrea said.

"Well, fair is a four-letter work that starts with *f*, and this whole situation is fucked up."

People were staring as they walked by, and Andrea did not want to have this conversation here. "Can we not talk about it right now," she said, almost pleading. "Let's go back to my office and we can—"

"No. I have to get to the control room. Don't bother to lower yourself and show me the way. I can find it."

Andrea was stunned. Granted, she didn't know Kenner at all, but she certainly was passionate about what she believed in and not afraid to say it. She watched Kenner move almost gracefully down the hall. She didn't swagger, but her stride was confident. Confident in her abilities, and if the second looks from more than a few heads turning were any indication, herself as well. Someone bumped Andrea's shoulder, bringing her to her senses. She quickly looked around to get her bearings and continued in the opposite direction to the one Kenner had gone. She needed to get to the control room, but she had to stop at her office first.

The door closed behind her, Andrea leaned against it. What had just happened? One minute the morning briefing had just ended, and the next Kenner was walking away, a tornado in her wake. Andrea's hands shook. The entire scene in Barry's office was unreal. Kenner had sucked up to him like a pro and, if Andrea would admit it to herself, was quite good at it.

From the minute Barry had asked to see Kenner, she'd been on edge. No, that wasn't right. From the minute she'd walked into the conference room and Kenner had shook her hand yesterday, she'd been on edge. She had no idea what Kenner would say to Barry, but if it was anything like the riot act she'd read her earlier this morning, she'd be up shit creek. The politeness had lasted only until they got out of his office. That was the Kenner she knew. She was feisty, outspoken, and gutsy.

"Andrea, they need you in the control room." The knock and accompanying message startled her.

"On the way." She was grateful her voice didn't betray her emotion. The control room. Her favorite place in the world, the place she couldn't wait to get to everyday and had to drag herself away from at night. It was where her thoughts were clear and her confidence never wavered. But now Kenner was there, and she'd seen her reaction to the words exchanged in Barry's office and in the hall. Uncharacteristically, she had to pull herself together. She smoothed the fabric of her shirt where it tucked into her pants and took a deep breath. Then she opened the door and went to work.

Chapter Thirteen

T-minus 08:13:12:09

The burning on the back of Kenner's neck was incessant. After her little tirade in the hall outside Haven's office, she found her way to the command center. The digital clock at the bottom of the screen reminded her that she'd been staring at the screen in front of her for the past three hours, and for most of that time she could tell Andrea was looking at her. She had no idea why and frankly didn't care. She was here for a short period of time; then she'd be on her way and never have to deal with the uptight Andrea or the ass Haven ever again.

She worked for Quantum so she wouldn't have to put up with this kind of shit for long. She could move on after she solved NASA's problem. After graduating she'd worked with a very large company, where she quickly witnessed so much back-stabbing, idea-stealing, and political crap she couldn't wait to get out. She was here at NASA to do a job, not stroke egos and take shit from people not nearly as smart as she was, or from anyone for that matter. Bosses like Andrea's were self-centered, egotistical, and more often than not intimidated by people who knew more than they did. Especially if that person was a woman.

Her stomach growled, and she decided this was as good a time as any to grab a bite. She stood and stretched her arms above her head, then arched her back. The snap, crackle, and pop in it, caused by sitting too long, sounded awful but felt fabulous. Touching her elbows together behind her back, she turned at the waist first to the left, then to right, repeating the action ten times. She dropped her chin to her chest, then to the left, right, and dropped her head back, each time counting to fifteen. She set the timer on her watch to ring on the half hour every hour she was working, and then she made herself get up and complete these same exercises. Without this routine she had horrible headaches and pains in her arms and could barely turn her head from side to side. Her stretches complete, she slid the chair under the desk and headed toward the door, all the while feeling Andrea's eyes on her.

What was up with that, Kenner wondered as she made her way through the maze of halls toward the cafeteria. A brunette with large breasts winked at her as she passed. Kenner turned her head and watched the tight butt in the short skirt continue down the hall. "Very nice," she said quietly, then looked around hoping no one had overheard.

She was finishing her burger when a wonderful scent drifted through the air from somewhere behind her. She was just about to turn to locate its source when a voice said, "May I join you?" The winking brunette came up from behind, stopping in front of her. Kenner's day had definitely gone from shitty to optimistic.

"Certainly," Kenner answered, standing up and indicating the empty chair in front of her. She had learned how to treat a lady by watching the way her father treated her mother. He stood when she approached or left the table, always opened the door for her, and brought her flowers for absolutely no reason. He never missed a birthday, anniversary, or special occasion. If something made her mother happy, he did it. If she wanted something, he bought it for her when she least expected it. And even after twenty-nine years, his eyes still lit up when she entered the room.

Last month had been their thirtieth wedding anniversary, and Kenner had gone home for the party. Her oldest sister had organized everything and, with Kenner and her other five siblings, had joined fifty of her parents' friends in celebration. Even with this display of obvious love and devotion, and the happy marriages of her four older brothers, Kenner had no desire to follow in their footsteps.

"Thanks," the brunette said, settling in. She extended her hand. "I'm Susie."

Kenner took the offered hand and held it a bit longer than straight women would. "Kenner," she replied, the familiar tingling starting between her legs.

"You're new here," Susie said, placing her napkin in her lap. It was more a statement than a question.

"Second day." Kenner liked what she saw sitting across from her at the small table. "I take it this is a social call?"

"Why do you ask that?" Susie placed her napkin in her lap.

"Because when you introduced yourself, you only used your first name." Susie looked puzzled. "Everyone I've met so far has been Jack Stevens, Booster; Rob Jazinski, Medical; and Paul Cooler, Gyro," she said, naming just a few of the people she'd met so far.

Susie understood. "Definitely a social call." She smiled and showed very white teeth. "Are you answering?"

Kenner liked Susie's straightforward, no-nonsense directness. She held her gaze for a few seconds. "Yes."

Susie's eyes sparkled. "How long are you here for?"

Susie glanced at her chest and Kenner lost track of the conversation.

"Your badge, it's temporary," Susie said, explaining her question.

Kenner tipped her badge up so she could see it. The large T behind her headshot indicated her employment status. "Does it matter?"

"Depends."

"On?"

"My plan of attack."

It was Kenner's turn to be confused. "Your plan of attack?"

"Yes, my plan of attack." Susie took a bite of her salad and chewed, then sipped from her soda.

Kenner prompted her, interested by Susie's approach. "Go on."

"Well, if you're going to be here for a few weeks or longer, I'd ask you to dinner a few times, maybe a movie or out for a drink. You understand, get-to-know-you kind of things."

"And if I'm not?" The tingling between her legs now was starting to demand attention.

"Then I'd ask if you were interested and want to get together for some no-strings, no-drama fun."

Holy cow, Kenner thought. Numerous women had propositioned her in various ways, but none had ever been as straightforward as Susie. She revised her day from shitty to optimistic to fabulous. "I'm working on an issue, and as soon as it's solved I'll be on my way."

"Are you local?"

"No, actually, I live in Atlanta."

Susie's eyebrows rose, and Kenner knew exactly what she was thinking. Even better, she'd been saying to herself. She'd never see this woman again for the rest of her life. Most of the time Kenner preferred this kind of attachment. Hook-up was a more appropriate word. No strings, no obligations, no awkward moments when you stumbled into each other at a club or, God forbid, a business function. She absolutely loved sex and everything about it. The anticipation, the tension, the verbal and visual foreplay, the signal a woman gave off when she was aroused. All of it was enticing: the way a woman's eyes darkened, her skin flushed and heated, the whiff of arousal, the scent of desire.

However, sometimes she felt a little odd afterward. Looking across the dinner table at the woman with which she'd been completely naked, flat on her back, or any number of other positions, her hands and mouth on the most intimate places on her body, made her feel odd. It was the only word she could use to describe it. It wasn't embarrassment or shyness; it was just feeling odd. She didn't feel that way when she shared a pizza with women after a game of basketball, or racing around a mountain on a pair of cross-country skis, or even the time she was very sick and barfed all over someone's shoes. She didn't feel odd in those situations. What Susie was obviously offering would eliminate any of that, and Kenner jumped in with both feet.

"What did you have in mind?" she asked.

"Like I said, I thought maybe we could have some fun together. You're away from home, I'm here. Maybe I could show you around, kill some time together."

Susie might have been offering innocuous suggestions, but Kenner read between the lines. Not being one to beat around the bush either, she learned forward and whispered, "I'd rather just fuck you until you beg me to stop."

Susie dropped her fork and it clattered on her plate. All heads in the room turned their way. Kenner slowly leaned back, maintaining a relaxed position in her chair while Susie scrambled to pick up her fork and act like nothing had happened. But Kenner knew the statement had affected her. Her neck was flushed, and not due to embarrassment, and her large breasts were moving up and down much faster than they were when she first sat down. Kenner even detected a slight tremor in Susie's hands.

"Well." Susie cleared her throat, obviously trying to regain her composure. "The only thing I can say to that is ditto."

Kenner's smile had persuaded one of her exes to go home with her. She'd said it held a teasing promise of what was to come.

"There's only one small issue," Kenner said cautiously. She didn't want to screw up this opportunity.

"And that is?"

"I came in yesterday, and my hotel arrangements got all fucked up, and there's not a room open in town. So I'm bunking with a coworker and we're car-pooling."

Susie thought about that for a few seconds. "And?" She left the question hanging in the air between them.

"It might be complicated to get away." Jeez, she felt like she was making plans to sneak out of her bedroom window at her parents' house. She'd done that many times and never got caught, but this was a different situation altogether.

"Why? Do they expect you to work twenty-four hours a day?"

"No," but Kenner thought Andrea would probably prefer that.

"So what's the problem? Your free time is your own, isn't it?"

Kenner nodded. "Of course it is." She hoped she didn't sound defensive. "It's just this is complicated."

"You already said that." Susie was losing some of her I-want-to-fuck-you look. Kenner felt her evening start to slide into shit and couldn't think of a way to stop it. "Give me your number and I'll try to work something out," she said, grabbing for a lifeline.

Susie hesitated, and the throbbing between Kenner's legs disappeared. Shit, I do not need this, she thought. When she was about to give up and get up from the table, Susie recited her number. Kenner jotted it on a napkin, not sure if she was thankful or annoyed. Annoyed at herself for not ditching Andrea and her uptight ass and standard operating procedures and have some fun. Let off some steam. Clear her head. That's what she needed. Not another night of working until midnight accompanied with another wordless drive back to Andrea's house. Maybe her hotel situation had been resolved. The way she and Andrea had snapped at each other, Kenner thought Andrea would be more than happy to tell her she was out of her house. That's what she'd have done if their roles were reversed.

Kenner watched her plans for tonight walk out the door.

Andrea sat across the room and watched Susie stroll away from Kenner. When she'd first approached Kenner, Andrea had lost her appetite. Susie had done the same thing to her several years ago, and even though it had been a long time since she'd been in the arms of a soft, warm woman, she'd respectfully declined. Susie hadn't taken the hint and had come back sniffing around several times before Andrea had told her very clearly to go away and stay away. She'd left Andrea alone, but from what she could tell, Susie was still very active in the hookup space. She didn't fault Susie or think she was a tramp or whatever the phrase was these days.

When she thought about it, she almost envied her and her ability to go after whatever or, more precisely, whomever she wanted.

So why had she felt angry when Susie sat down at Kenner's table? It wasn't any of her business what Kenner did in her spare time. Wasn't any of her business who she slept with and whether she'd just met them or had known them for months. Kenner was an adult. She exhibited confidence and experience with women, and with her looks and charm, she'd obviously had plenty of practice. Andrea had no doubt Kenner could handle Susie, and by the looks of their body language and the heated looks they were exchanging across the table, handle was definitely going to happen.

Andrea frowned on interwork relationships. More often than not, when they went bad they were sticky and ugly, and one of the players always came out the loser. But Kenner wasn't her employee, even though she was part of this mission. Andrea didn't have any say in her work habits or her work relationships other than the fact that whatever she did could not interfere with the main reason she was here.

Andrea couldn't help but watch the two interact from across the room. It always surprised her that Susie's approach was more often than not successful. It appeared that in a very short period of time she would have another notch in her NASA belt.

When Andrea returned to the control room, Kenner had her feet on her desk, twiddling a pencil between her fingers as the data rolled across the screen in front of her.

"What are you doing?" Andrea asked from over Kenner's left shoulder. Her tone was harsh.

"Following the trail of these commands," Kenner answered, nodding toward the screen. Kenner didn't change her position, nor did she turn around to look at Andrea.

"It doesn't look like that's what you're doing."

"It doesn't matter what it looks like I'm doing but what I am actually doing."

"Well, it doesn't appear that way to me and certainly not to everyone else." Andrea was more than a little annoyed at this point.

"Why are you worried about what everyone else thinks?" Kenner asked.

"Because everyone has a vested interest in this mission."

"And I don't?"

"Well," Andrea said. She moved and was now standing beside her. "Look at yourself. Does this say hard at work," Andrea said, pointing at her body.

"Yes, it does," Kenner answered, jotting a few notes on the pad balanced precariously on her outstretched legs. "Just because it happens to be in a different language than what everyone is used to around here doesn't mean it doesn't have the same definition." Kenner still hadn't taken her eyes from the screen. She glanced at her watch and made a few more notes.

"I heard you had company for lunch," Andrea asked. Jesus, why did stupid things keep coming put her mouth when she was around Kenner?

"I see the grapevine in alive and well at the Johnson Space Center."

"Susie is…" Andrea paused, looking for the right word.

"Attractive?" Kenner supplied the adjective in a helpful tone.

"Among other things," Andrea said sarcastically.

"I'm sorry. She told me she wasn't involved with anyone. She certainly didn't tell me it was you."

"It's not me. I'm definitely not involved with Susie," Andrea replied vehemently. Her personal life was just that—personal. She never brought it to the office.

"But you want to be?"

"In her dreams," Andrea said, with even more force and conviction.

"Then what's the problem? We're both of age." Kenner stood and started the stretching routine Andrea had seen her complete every hour or so.

"I don't think office romances are a good idea," Andrea said stiffly.

"I don't do romance," Kenner replied. "But two consenting adults spending time together with no expectations and strings can be very refreshing. Not to say how it relieves stress." Kenner raised her eyebrows several times a lá Groucho Marx.

Andrea took a step toward her and leaned forward. "I am not having this conversation with you." Her voice was low and came through clenched teeth.

Kenner took a step forward, forcing Andrea to lean back. "You started it."

Andrea was fuming. "Get back to work," she growled, trying to save face. When she turned to leave she saw at least four heads quickly turn to look at their screens. Fucking great, she had an audience.

Several hours later Andrea was finalizing a report when Kenner approached. Jesus, what now, she asked herself. She didn't want another scene. Fuck, she hadn't wanted that scene earlier in the first fat place. What in the hell had gotten into her? She steeled herself for whatever Kenner had to say. She kept telling herself to hold it together, something she'd never had a problem with before. She put her pen down when Kenner stopped in front of her desk.

"Have you heard anything about my hotel arrangements?" Kenner asked, no sign of the earlier antagonism in her voice.

"Yes." Andrea was relieved the subject wasn't another controversial one. "I received an email from travel a few minutes ago. Unfortunately it's status quo, at least for another day or so."

"Shit," Kenner mumbled under her breath but loud enough that she heard it.

Andrea opened her mouth to make a comment, but Kenner held both hands up as if in surrender. "I'll be ready to go when you are." Then she turned and walked back to her workstation.

CHAPTER FOURTEEN

T-minus 07:23:42:37

The ride to her house was as silent as it had been the night before. Andrea didn't know what to say. She was terrible at small talk. She could talk work all day, but the conversation she and Kenner had earlier today had absolutely nothing to do with work. She didn't know whether to bring it up or just let it go. As tempted as she was to let it go, she regretted her comments.

"I want to apologize for what I said earlier today. It was unprofessional, and I guarantee it will never happen again," Andrea said in a rush, needing to get the words out. For some reason this conversation made her more nervous than any other time she could remember. Probably because it was personal, and, like Kenner had said about herself, Andrea didn't do personal. She gripped the steering wheel even tighter when Kenner didn't immediately respond.

Finally Kenner said, "Let's just chalk it up to a stressful situation. And you're right. It is none of your business, and I accept your apology."

Andrea turned her head to the side and expelled a lung full of air.

"Are you that nervous about talking to me?" Kenner asked.

Andrea kept both eyes on the road but could see Kenner out of the corner of her eye. Not only was Kenner looking at her but had turned in her seat so she was almost facing her.

"No, of course not."

"Then what would you call it?" Kenner asked, her tone light.

"I don't know." She answered honestly. "Uncomfortable, maybe."

"Why?"

Andrea gritted her teeth. Kenner was not going to drop this subject. "Because it never should have happened in the first place. You're right. Your life is none of my business. When I made it mine I was stepping over the line."

"And you don't often step over the line," Kenner said.

"Actually never," Andrea replied, trying not to be defensive. "The complexity of what we do every day doesn't allow for variance. We have no room for error. If we do, it could be disastrous." God, she sounded like a recorded message.

Even in the dark she could feel Kenner's penetrating eyes on her. That was one of the first things she'd noticed about her. Her eyes were an unusual shade of green, especially with her dark hair and complexion. It was as if Kenner could see right through her eyes, directly into her head to what she was thinking. Andrea knew that wasn't possible; however, with a woman as brilliant as Kenner, it wouldn't have surprised her.

Kenner did surprise her when she let the subject drop. Andrea knew she'd dodged the question. Kenner was asking about her personally, not her personal life, and Kenner knew she had completely avoided it. Andrea was safe and secure in her work. In the routine, in the analytical, predictable thought process behind everything. That was her, her life, what she did, who she was, sometimes seven days a week. Of course she'd be more comfortable there than anywhere else. And if Kenner didn't like it, then too bad. She wasn't her shrink, and if Kenner expected that they were going to have some kind of touching Hallmark-card moment, she needed to think again.

"I don't have anything at my house to eat. Do you want to stop somewhere? There's steak, Chinese, Thai, and Mexican between here and there."

Kenner shifted in the seat, putting her feet back on the floorboard, turning those penetrating eyes away from her.

"Sure, how about steak?"

"All right," she said, looking for the familiar sign on the road in front of her.

Andrea couldn't believe Kenner could put away such a huge amount of food and still be able to maintain her thin figure. Three slices of bread, then salad, then an eight-ounce rib eye, a loaded baked potato, and a heaping pile of freshly steamed broccoli. She, on the other hand, had barely touched her salad and ate only one of her steak kabobs and none of her rice.

Kenner had kept up the conversation through most of the meal, discussing the mission or innocuous topics. When she steered too close to anything personal, Andrea shifted the subject.

"Have you ever been to China?" Kenner asked after giving the waitress her order for dessert.

"No, I haven't."

"It's one of the most fascinating places in the world. The masses of people, the crowds, the immense wealth right next to abject poverty are unbelievable."

"When did you go?"

"Four or five years ago. We were over there on business and took a few days afterward to play tourist. Our guide took us to an authentic Chinese restaurant, and you know how it is when company comes to town, especially foreign visitors, and you go to the most expensive place that reflects your local cuisine?"

Andrea nodded, not because she'd experienced this, but because it was obviously the right thing to say. She left the entertaining to Barry and the higher-ups.

"It was the most disgusting meal I've ever had in my life."

Andrea's heart skipped when Kenner smiled as she told her story. As a matter of fact, her heart skipped quite a bit during dinner—when Kenner laughed, used her hands to express herself, or just when she looked at her.

"Our guide ordered for us, and pretty quick here comes this platter with this fish on it, complete with the head and tail. It had been gutted, but I swear it was still alive. More plates came out and I had no idea what they were. Everything was absolutely fascinating and disgusting at the same time. I don't like sushi, but this wasn't even that. It was maybe boiled or seared for all of two or three seconds, and it was gross. I didn't eat any of it, just moved my fork back and forth to my mouth. Everyone else ate it, and they were sicker than hell the next day. We had to delay our return because they couldn't get out of bed."

Andrea couldn't help but chuckle at Kenner's story. The way she phrased it, the tone of her voice, and the expression on her face were enjoyable, and she hadn't enjoyed herself in such a long time.

"But the worst is when it happens on a business trip. Then it's not polite not to eat. It's a sign of disrespect, and all hopes of getting anything done on that trip, or maybe even ever, are dead. That's my definition of misery. One meal I had to excuse myself four times to go to the bathroom and puke."

Andrea grimaced, her stomach turning a bit in sympathy. Kenner's dessert arrived, a three-inch brownie topped with a large scoop of vanilla ice cream melting on top. She offered her a bite, but Andrea shook her head. Chocolate that late in the evening gave her weird dreams, and sharing part of a meal was far too intimate.

Kenner told several more stories of her adventures. She'd been all over the world. She'd experienced different places, different cultures, different people. Andrea had never been outside the United States. She hadn't been to Cancun or even Rocky Point in Mexico. The sparkle in Kenner's eyes when she talked about her friends and coworkers and described how it was like to have a beer in a local pub made Andrea suddenly feel a little hollow. My God, she was thirty-six years old and hadn't been anywhere or done anything.

The check arrived as Kenner put her fork down on the now-empty plate. Andrea reached for it at the same time Kenner did.

"I can get this," Kenner said.

"No," Andrea replied, sliding the folder onto the seat beside her. "This is on NASA."

"Well, in that case, how about an after-dinner cocktail?"

Kenner laughed before she could answer. "I'm just kidding," she said, wiping her mouth with her napkin. "This was delicious, thank you." She folded her napkin and laid it on the table beside her plate, signaling she was done. "Ugh," she groaned. "I'm stuffed to the brim. I can't remember when I've had a meal so good.

Kenner had been a little apprehensive when Andrea had pulled into the parking lot of the dilapidated building. She'd decided not to say anything and give Andrea the benefit of the doubt. The Wagon Wheel was definitely a little hole-in-the-wall joint off the beaten path, the kind of place you'd never enter unless you knew how good the food was.

She hadn't been quite sure what to expect when they walked in. But between the food, ambiance, music, and Andrea, she'd been surprised all the way around. Andrea was making an effort, but obviously she didn't know what to say, so Kenner had pretty much led the conversation and picked the topics. She had noticed that when they walked in everyone had looked at the latest entry into their local watering hole, and she definitely hadn't missed the fact that the men couldn't keep their eyes off Andrea as they strolled to their table.

Andrea definitely was easy on the eyes sitting across the table over a meal; however, she never really relaxed. She was very smart, literate, and extremely well read. Kenner hadn't met too many people that were as technically competent as Andrea but had read the complete works of Shakespeare, Hawthorne, and Agatha Christie.

When Kenner had asked about her family or anything personal, Andrea gave vague answers and quickly changed the subject. After a few times Kenner got the message and didn't go down that path again.

"Do you always eat that much?" Andrea asked, putting the key in the ignition and starting the car.

"Every chance I get," she replied. Andrea looked at her with an are-you-kidding-me expression. "But I don't get many chances, so when I do I take full advantage of it."

Andrea smiled, shook her head, and put the car in reverse. As she turned around to look out the rear window, her shirt pulled tightly across her breasts. At the risk of being busted again, Kenner peeked. Andrea's breasts were what Kenner would describe as no more than a handful, which in her opinion was perfect. You can only put so much in your hands or your mouth. Speaking about putting things in her mouth, she realized she hadn't thought about the missed opportunity with Susie since entering the restaurant.

She shifted her eyes back to the road before Andrea was aware she was leering at her chest, wishing for a button or two to pop. Andrea put the car in drive, looked both ways, and pulled out of the parking lot.

"Is your neighborhood safe?" Kenner asked when they pulled into Andrea's garage.

"Excuse me?"

Kenner closed her door before repeating her question. "Your neighborhood. Is it safe to walk around the block? I need to exercise some of this food off."

Andrea looked at her watch and frowned. "It's eleven fifteen."

"Is that a yes or a no?"

"It's kind of late for a walk."

"Then come with me."

"What?" Andrea asked, apparently surprised.

"Come with me. There's safety in numbers, you know," Kenner said, toying with her. Andrea looked completely dumbfounded and was kind of cute without her serious face.

"Are you crazy?" Andrea asked, obviously thinking she was.

"About what? Wanting to go for a walk or asking you to come with me?"

"Both. It's far too late to be walking around at night, even with two of us. I have a treadmill in one of the bedrooms you can use. That'll have to do," she said, ending the conversation.

❖

After showing Kenner where the treadmill was, Andrea took a shower. The evening had gotten off to a rocky start but had ended up pretty enjoyable. Not only was Kenner brilliant, she was also quick and witty and had a great sense of humor. Andrea's stomach fluttered when she thought about Kenner's laugh. It was full and not the slightest self-conscious, and when she laughed along with her, Andrea had felt almost free. It had been a long time since she'd laughed, and she hadn't realized how much she'd missed it.

She'd been working nonstop for the past five months leading up to the liftoff of the *Explorer*. She'd lost touch with the few friends she had, her work taking up almost every minute of her life. But even before things got absolutely crazy, she hadn't made time to go out. She couldn't remember the last movie she'd seen or the last time she'd read anything other than a technical manual or report. She finished her shower, pulled on a pair of loose pajama bottoms, a T-shirt with MIT ALUMNI embroidered across the front, and her robe. She would check on Kenner before she went to bed.

The sound of feet pounding on the treadmill told her Kenner must have decided to run instead of walk. As she strolled down the hall, Andrea wondered where Kenner found the energy. She was exhausted, both mentally and physically, and it was all she could do to make it down the hall to her room instead of collapse on the couch. She froze in the doorway of the room.

Kenner was running fast, her arms and legs pumping. A pair of very, very short bright-green running shorts and a contrasting sports bra displayed her body, with almost nothing left to the imagination. And holy God, she looked good. Her chest was covered in sweat and glowed with strength and power. The muscles in her legs were well defined and her stomach perfectly flat. My God, Andrea thought, she could be in a magazine ad and I would buy whatever she was selling. Kenner was an exquisite example of a woman in action, and Andrea couldn't do anything other than stare. She stood transfixed as Kenner increased her speed and breathed harder.

Andrea didn't know how long she'd been standing there, but when Kenner reduced the speed on the treadmill and reached for the towel draped over the controls, their eyes met. A bolt of something vaguely familiar shot through Andrea's body and straight between her legs. Kenner's chest was heaving, her breathing fast. Andrea felt hers moving in time with it. Kenner's eyes darkened, and she pulled an earbud out of her right ear.

Andrea knew she should say something, preferably good night, or do something like hand Kenner the water bottle on the table next to her, but she really wanted to tell Kenner just how magnificent she thought her body was, then turn, run down the hall, and lock herself in her bedroom.

"I'm sorry," Kenner said, hitting the stop button and stepping off the slowing belt. "Am I keeping you awake?"

Andrea couldn't form a coherent thought as Kenner walked toward her, toweling the sweat off her face. Words wouldn't form in her brain, and the command to close her mouth didn't work either.

"Andrea?" Kenner asked. "Are you all right?"

Kenner searched her face, and when her eyes came back to hers, the pounding between her legs intensified. Holy Mother of

God, she's beautiful, she heard a little voice in her head say. It was also telling her to take four steps forward, take Kenner in her arms, and kiss her—long, hard, and forever.

"Andrea?" Kenner asked again, this time more forcefully.

"Do it. Do it now," the voice in her head said. "You won't be sorry." Andrea shook her head, trying to clear the voice. "Do it. Grab her, pin her to the wall, and kiss her."

"No," Andrea said forcefully and took a step backward. Kenner froze mid-step and put her hands up, signaling she wasn't a threat.

"Andrea? What is it?" she asked, looking puzzled and obviously confused.

Andrea realized she'd spoken out loud and suddenly wanted to crawl between the seams in the carpet and disappear forever. Actually she wanted this entire scene to have not happened. What should she do now? Why was she always trying to figure out what to do or say when she was around Kenner? God, it was like she was fifteen again.

"It's nothing," she said, her voice betraying how affected she was by seeing Kenner, her half-naked body covered in sweat. "I was talking to the voice in my head."

Kenner looked at her for quite a few moments before finally asking, "What was it telling you?"

Grab her, pin her to the wall, and kiss her. That's what it was telling her. But instead she managed to say, "That I should tell you that you shouldn't work out so late in the evening. You'll never get to sleep." *Good God, where had that come from?*

Kenner surely knew she was full of shit, and Andrea tried to cover her inane remarks by adding, "But it's none of my business. I was just going to ask if you needed anything before I went to bed." *Like a kiss, or for me to lick the sweat off your upper lip. Or maybe that drip disappearing between your breasts.* Andrea tensed. If Kenner did one thing, made one move toward her, said one thing encouraging, she wouldn't be able to hold herself back. As it was, she was struggling to stand still.

Kenner studied her for more than a few seconds, and Andrea was thankful she couldn't read her mind. "Stop being a coward. Do it," the voice said again. "You want to and you know it, and judging by the look on her face, she wouldn't say no." Finally it was Kenner who stepped back.

"No, nothing, thanks," Kenner said, and Andrea couldn't even remember her question.

"I'll just grab a quick shower and go to bed myself. Thanks for letting me use this," Kenner continued, pointing behind her. "It was just what I needed." Kenner's eyes narrowed and darkened. "Oh, and I never have trouble falling asleep after a workout," she said confidently.

Andrea's stomach dropped, as did her mouth. The innuendo was as plain as the accompanying expression on Kenner's face. Before she could make any more of a fool of herself than she already had, she said good night. As much as Andrea wanted to run down the hall, she forced herself to walk. It was after she closed and locked the door that her knees gave out. She slid to the floor and dropped her face in her hands. What in the fuck had just happened, and WTF had just happened to her?

Kenner watched Andrea walk away. She obviously couldn't get out of here fast enough. "What was that all about?" she asked before turning the cap on her water bottle and taking a swig. Something was definitely wrong, but she wasn't sure what. Andrea had said she could use the treadmill, and that's all she'd been doing when she came in. Granted, she was pounding away and had just crossed the five-mile mark when she'd reduced the speed to start her cool-down.

Kenner wiped her face with a towel and saw that her hand was shaking. It couldn't have been from her workout. She hated running on sterile treadmills, but that had been little more than her normal warm-up before going for a much-longer run. Maybe she was just a little out of shape. Running relaxed her and cleared her head, and she tried to do it at least three or four times a week. But she'd been on vacation for a week before getting Andrea's call. However, that was only three days ago, and she'd been relaxing and clearing her head in other, more pleasurable ways than churning out miles.

She wiped down the treadmill, gathered up her things, and turned off the light. She hesitated in front of Andrea's bedroom and leaned her head toward the door. She didn't know what she was listening for, but when she didn't hear anything she knocked softly.

"Andrea?" Her voice wasn't very loud in case Andrea was sleeping, but she doubted it. As agitated as she'd been, no way could she be asleep by now.

"Andrea?" she called again. When she didn't answer, Kenner continued down the hall to the guest room. She showered quickly, the cool water refreshing on her heated skin. She didn't bother to put on any clothes, but just slid naked between the sheets.

❖

Andrea leaned against the counter and closed her eyes. The smell of fresh coffee dripping relaxed her a little, but she was still keyed up. Last night she had barely been able to pull herself together and get to her room when Kenner had knocked on her door. She'd sensed when Kenner had stopped at her door and didn't know if she was relieved or disappointed that she didn't insist she answer the door. If she had, Andrea didn't know if she'd have had the strength to send her away. The voice in her head certainly would have been encouraging her to invite her in.

Jesus, what had gotten in to her last night? It wasn't as if she hadn't seen a half-naked woman before. And Kenner wasn't even that. She was dressed like any number of the women in Andrea's gym and was even more covered than a few. Granted, Andrea went to the gym, did her workout, and went home. She didn't look at the other women or their bodies, and she certainly never ogled them like she had Kenner's. Dear God, it was like she was dying of thirst and only Kenner could quench it. She'd never been as rattled by another woman as she had by the sight of Kenner's sweaty body last night. She just had to get through today and the next few days until they fixed this problem, and then she could continue with her life. It was just that simple. She'd willed her way through tougher, more challenging situations, and this was merely one more.

Andrea carried a mug of coffee and knocked on the guest-room door. It took only a few moments before Kenner told her to come in.

❖

Kenner was scooting up to lean against the headboard, and when the sheet slid down, Andrea knew the day couldn't get much worse. Oh, my God! Kenner was naked, and her breasts were more beautiful than what Andrea had imagined them to be last night. Kenner calmly pulled the sheet up and covered herself.

"Sorry," Kenner said, tucking the sheet more tightly around her. "I guess I wasn't as decent as I thought I was," she said apologetically.

Andrea could only stare at the pristine white sheet that covered Kenner's magnificent chest. A tattoo Andrea couldn't quite make out peeked out just above the sheet over her right breast, and Andrea wanted to walk, not run, over and slowly tug the sheet down to reveal it in its entirety.

"Andrea?" Kenner asked.

"Oh, yeah, sorry," she said, forcing her eyes up across Kenner's naked shoulders, up her neck, past full lips, and into her eyes. Kenner's knowing eyes. Andrea felt a blush creep up her neck and chose to ignore it. There was nothing she could do about it anyway. "No problem," she said, somehow crossing the room and intending to set the cup on the nightstand. She was afraid if she handed it to Kenner, she would be dangerously close to the body that had danced in her dreams. What she didn't count on was how the sheet shifted when Kenner reached for the cup instead.

Andrea had two choices. Move closer so Kenner didn't need to lean forward any more or stay where she was and let the chips fall where they may, as the saying went. But it wasn't chips that would fall. It would be the sheet, followed by her resolve to get through this morning and every morning until Kenner left her house.

"Is that for me?" Kenner asked, pointing to the cup in her hand.

Andrea's melting brain caught the lifeline, and she stepped closer and handed Kenner the cup. Their fingers touched, and a shaft of heat traveled up her arm, crisscrossing inside her chest, and settled firmly between her legs. Oh, God, she didn't need this.

Her eyes dropped to Kenner's chest, and the pulsing in her clit demanded attention. She released the cup and forced her eyes back to Kenner's, and what she saw took her breath away. Her eyes were a darker shade of green, the flame of desire unmistakable. *Oh God, I can't do this. Please, I can't do this.*

"Thank you," Kenner said, and Andrea jumped at the opportunity to move back a few steps. It gave her some breathing room, but that went out the window when she saw Kenner's confident, knowing smile. The blush she felt now was one of anger, not embarrassment.

"We need to leave in thirty minutes," she said, hurriedly trying to gather herself. One minute she was almost overcome with desire, and the next instant she was furious. She couldn't deal with much more of this emotional flip-flop.

"I said thank you," Kenner said.

"I just brought you coffee. No big deal," she said defensively and turned to leave.

"I meant thank you for looking at me the way you did."

Andrea pivoted and glared at Kenner. "For looking at you the way I did?"

"Yes, I liked it, and obviously you did too."

Now Andrea was really angry. Her response was not meant to be a question, and she said so through clenched teeth.

"Sounded like one to me. Like you didn't understand my meaning," Kenner added and didn't move to raise the sheet that had dropped again.

"I know exactly what your meaning was, and I'm not interested."

"That's not what your body said and not what I saw," Kenner said.

"Then you need to have your eyes checked. Susie's the one who's interested in a quick, no-strings-attached roll in the sheets. I'm not." God, she sounded pathetic.

"I never said it would be quick."

Kenner's voice was husky with morning wake-up and desire, and Andrea's pulse raced even faster. It was suddenly hard to take a breath. No, she thought, it would definitely not be quick with Kenner.

"Thirty minutes. Get dressed." For the second time in a few hours she forced her legs to take her out the door.

Andrea looked at her watch for the third time in as many minutes when Kenner emerged from the guest room. Today she wore a pair of khakis and a long-sleeved navy T-shirt with a logo of a turtle on the front. Andrea picked up her keys and briefcase and headed toward the garage, still fuming.

"I'm sorry if I embarrassed you," Kenner said, surprising her.

"You didn't. I'm just not interested." She pushed the button to open the garage door much harder than necessary.

"Andrea..." Kenner started to say more.

Andrea didn't want to hear it. As a matter of fact she didn't want to even acknowledge there was something there. Kenner had seen it. Anybody who wasn't blind could have seen it, and she was embarrassed that she hadn't been able to keep her emotions under wraps. She hadn't slept much last night because she was thinking about her reaction to seeing Kenner all sweaty and magnificent. As much as she wanted to, she couldn't deny that she was attracted to her. Actually, she would describe her urge as much more than attraction. She'd use words like lust, desire, and passion. But she was stronger than her desires. She always had been, and that wasn't going to change now. Too much was at stake.

"I mean it, Kenner. I'm not interested. Do I need to make it any clearer?" she asked in her no-bullshit, mission-director voice.

CHAPTER FIFTEEN

T-minus 07:07:18:49

Barry was waiting for Andrea inside her office. Great, just what she needed, she thought, plastering a welcoming smile on her face. "Good morning, Barry. Do we have a meeting?" she asked, knowing they didn't.

"What's the status?" he asked, not even bothering to return her greeting. When had he become such a dick?

What a stupid-ass question. It was obvious she'd just arrived. She told him as much. "I haven't had a chance to read the logs from last night, but since my phone didn't ring telling me otherwise, I would surmise that things are status quo." Judging by the look on Barry's face, that wasn't the answer he was looking for. "But give me ten minutes and I can give you a complete update," she added quickly.

What had gotten into her? She respected Barry and his authority over this mission and never would have answered him like she just had. Actually she never would have had to because she was always in before Barry and was able to brief him or anyone else on any aspect of the mission at any time.

Her lack of sleep and the constant aggravation of dealing with Kenner had her on edge. She wasn't herself, and as much as she told herself to get it together, she was still repeating that mantra.

Never had she been so distracted that it took any more than telling herself to get her head back in the game. Her mind seemed to have a mind of its own. At least the voice in her head had quieted. God, she needed all this to be over, now.

Barry asked her a few more questions, and as soon as he left her office Andrea hurried to the conference room. She was never late to the morning briefing and didn't want to start now.

She wasn't even ten minutes into the meeting, and no matter how hard she tried to stop them, Andrea's eyes kept returning to Kenner. This was the third morning briefing with Kenner in attendance, and she sat in a different chair each day. The other members of her team always sat in the same places, and it was interesting to watch them when their usual seat was occupied. This morning Kenner was lounging at the other end of the table directly across from her.

Given the way Kenner was looking at her, Andrea was afraid she could read her mind. She was probably laughing at her embarrassment and overreaction of this morning. Just thinking about Kenner's breasts and how good she looked lying naked in her guest bed made her stomach begin to tingle. No, Andrea thought, she was probably trying to figure out how to slip away and get Susie in bed. From what she'd seen yesterday and knowing Susie's reputation, she was certain Kenner would have absolutely no trouble. But what did she care? And why did she keep asking herself that question?

"Andrea?"

Andrea almost jumped, and she realized everyone was looking at her, including Kenner. She felt a flush creep up her neck. "I'm sorry. I was thinking about something else. What was the question?"

Andrea cringed inside when the question was repeated. She never lost track of a conversation, daydreamed in a meeting, zoned out, or lost interest. Never. Ever. And everyone in the room except Kenner knew it. What in the hell was happening to her?

Ten awkward minutes later she adjourned the meeting. Everyone filed out like good little solders, but Kenner remained. *Great, just great.*

"Are you okay?" Kenner asked, approaching her.

"Of course." Even if Andrea were on her death bed, she'd never say otherwise.

"You looked a little distracted," Kenner said, obviously trying to get her to confess.

"No, not at all," Andrea lied. "I'm just concerned that we're not making any significant headway. That's all." That part was true.

Kenner looked at her for several moments. Her eyes roamed across her face, and Andrea's pulse started to race. She had to play it cool, keep it together. That was easy enough to do. It was a simple case of mind over matter. She always accomplished what she set her mind to, and why would this be any different? But you can't erase something you've seen, especially when it was as stunningly beautiful as Kenner's bare skin and breasts. The sight of them was burned into her brain like a brand.

Kenner's penetrating eyes made Andrea uncomfortable. She forced herself not to squirm or be the first to look away. She was in charge and had to maintain control of the situation. "Is there anything else?" she asked, praying the answer was no.

Kenner must have been giving serious thought to her answer because it took a long time for her to respond. "We'll get it," she said, referring to why she was here in the first place. Her face relaxed its intense scrutiny. "It'll take a little time, but we'll get it."

Andrea breathed a sigh of relief as Kenner walked out the door.

❖

"Bullshit," Kenner mumbled as she strolled down the hall. Her conversation with Andrea pushed her bullshit meter off the charts. She'd seen the look in Andrea's eyes last night. She knew the unmistakable signs of raw desire. She'd seen the way Andrea's body responded when she saw her in bed this morning. Kenner hadn't intended for the sheet to slide down, but gravity being what it is... She wasn't shy, and to quickly grab the sheet and cover herself would have caused more attention to the situation than doing nothing, or at least that's what she told herself.

Kenner had wanted to reach out and pull Andrea into bed with her, but she hadn't. The threat that Andrea would slap her and throw her out of her house and this job was deterrent enough. Kenner instinctively knew Andrea wanted her, but no way was she going to put herself out there to get knocked down. There were many, many other fish in the sea. She pulled out her phone and pushed the number next to Susie's name.

The day flew by, and Kenner finally felt like she was starting to make progress. She was beginning to fully understand the situation and knew the solution would jump out at her in the next few days. Her neck hurt, her back ached, and the data in front of her was starting to run together. She needed a break. She rolled her chair next to the man sitting in the workstation to her right.

"Hey, Mitchell."

"Yes," he answered, not looking up from his own data.

"Is there a place to blow off some steam around here? Like a gym or a track or something?"

"There's a basketball court just outside building twelve. Robertson in Purchasing has a ball under his desk. Two halls over behind the blue door."

Kenner thanked him and set out to find the aforementioned blue door.

The ball bounced off the end of the rim, and Kenner sprinted to catch it before it rolled off the court and into the mud. She didn't know how long she'd been shooting hoops, but she was breathing fast and her arms were getting tired, as evidenced by her missing her last several shots.

"What are you doing out here?" Andrea's angry voice came from behind her.

"Shooting hoops. Wanna join me?"

"You're shooting hoops?" Andrea asked, sounding incredulous.

"Yes," Kenner said. Her answer was pretty self-explanatory. She released another shot from the left of the basket, relieved the shot hit nothing but net. The last thing she wanted to do was to have to chase the ball down in front of Andrea. How embarrassing would that be?

She grabbed the ball and turned to face Andrea, who did not look happy. Her hands were on her hips, her feet shoulder-length apart. A scowl covered her face, and her eyes were dark. "Do you need something?"

Kenner wasn't done shooting, her thoughts only starting to clear and synthesize. Her brain worked best when it was relaxed. It was as if the absence of stimulation or data input made room for it to all come together. She'd determined the solution to her last two assignments while on the racquetball court at her apartment.

"I need you back at work."

"Did you find something?" she asked quickly, her pulse jumping.

"No, that's why *you're* here. Against my better judgment," she murmured after the fact.

"Is there a problem?"

"You are the problem," Andrea snapped.

"I thought you just said I was the solution. Make up your mind, Andrea." Kenner had no idea why she'd said that, but her well-earned relaxation had all but disappeared with Andrea's arrival.

"Seventeen men and women in the control room and another several dozen more are working on this problem. I don't see any of them out here shooting hoops."

"Not my problem they don't know how to relax." Kenner goaded her.

"Don't you think you should be inside working?" Andrea asked, not even trying to mask her sarcasm.

"No, but obviously you do."

"Yes, I do, and everyone else does as well."

"I don't care what they think." She had long ago stopped worrying about what people thought of her. After years of enduring teasing and taunting, Kenner had toughened her skin as a matter of survival. If it didn't matter, it couldn't hurt.

"I need—"

"Didn't we have this conversation yesterday? The one where you chastised me because I wasn't sitting in the ergonomically NASA regulated position. Well, this is same thing, and for the second time I don't need to explain myself to you. And I'm not going to." She sank another seventeen-footer with nothing but net. "So unless you're going to join me, I suggest you get off the court. You might get hurt. Never know when the ball will rebound off the rim at an odd angle." Kenner was furious but wasn't about to let Andrea see that she'd upset her.

Kenner ignored Andrea, or at least she let her think she was ignoring her, and sank a few more before transitioning to layups. Out of the corner of her eye she saw Andrea standing there, probably deciding what to do next. This was a classic power play, and Kenner didn't participate in that game. Finally Andrea turned and stormed back into the building, her body stiff. Kenner knew this wasn't over.

Andrea fumed as she stomped back to the door she'd come out not five minutes earlier. She'd walked over to the window in the control room to stretch her legs, and movement on the court below her had caught her attention. When she saw Kenner's workstation empty she'd reached the conclusion that she was on the court instead of in her seat.

Andrea hadn't expected Kenner's flip attitude but then again, after their earlier conversation, she wasn't surprised. She seethed because Kenner was right. They had had this conversation yesterday, but this situation was different. Why couldn't she see that? Andrea had a staff to keep focused, discipline to maintain, and a reputation to uphold. Kenner was undermining her just about every step of the way. This couldn't go on much longer, but she would never ask Barry to remove Kenner from the team.

Andrea simmered. Never in a million years would she admit that she couldn't control a team member. That would be career suicide. She'd worked too hard, trained too long for this snot-nosed, pompous little shit to throw her off track. It wouldn't happen. She would not let it happen.

Several people looked up as she reentered the control room, and she kept her expression neutral as she walked to her desk. She didn't need for anyone on her team to see how angry she was. And angry she was—at Kenner, but more at herself for letting Kenner get under her skin. No one had ever sparked her anger and frustration like this woman did. Was it her lackadaisical attitude? Her youth? Her confidence?

For a moment Andrea wondered if she might be jealous, then brushed the possibility off as ridiculous. After all, Kenner was brilliant, obviously worked and played hard, didn't care who knew she was gay, and added to all that, she had dynamite looks. She had her entire future in front of her.

Andrea suddenly felt old and tired. She'd single-mindedly driven herself so hard for so many years that she'd rarely taken a break. Her last vacation had been over two years ago, and she really hadn't had any choice. Her brother Stan was getting married, and her mother had threatened to disown her if she didn't show up for the full week of activities. Andrea had compromised and flown to San Francisco, where her brother and his fiancé were living, two days before and left the day after the wedding. Her friends had stopped calling her months ago and wouldn't even try to get in touch again for several more. Dinner with Kenner last night was the first time she'd eaten anywhere other than at her desk or in front of the TV in she didn't know how long.

When had her life become so one-dimensional? It probably always had been, but when had it become such a mess? And why did it always start to unravel when Kenner was around? Andrea was shaking her head to regain her focus when Kenner strolled in. Instead of returning to her workstation she headed toward her. Andrea's back tensed, ready for another battle. She wondered if this one would be of words or will.

"Any news on a hotel?"

That wasn't what Andrea had expected Kenner to say, and it took a moment for her to process the question. "Not that I'm aware of." Andrea had meant to send an email to the travel department but become sidetracked when she saw Kenner outside. "I know you're eager to get out of my house and have your own privacy. I'm sure Susie would appreciate it too."

Kenner's eyebrows rose. Hmm, Andrea thought. I read that one right.

"It would make things…uh…less complicated," Kenner admitted.

"Of course it would. Far be it from me to stand in the way of true love." *Jesus, where did that come from?*

"You know, Andrea, I'm beginning to think you have a problem with sex."

"Don't you dare even begin to assume you know anything about me," Andrea shot back, furious, but of course Kenner just stared at her and obviously wasn't about to let it drop.

"Or is it just that you have a problem with me having sex? No." Kenner paused and smiled. "I know. You have a problem with me having sex but just not with you."

Andrea fought the urge to jump up and slap the smug look off Kenner's face. Obviously that wasn't possible, but she did stand and step close to her. "I warned you, Kenner." She kept her voice low, but her words came out between clenched teeth.

"You started it, *again*," Kenner said. "I simply asked about a hotel room. You're the one who assumed sex was involved. But just to appease your prurient interest, yes, I do have plans for tonight. All night, as a matter of fact. But I do have enough class not to do whatever I have in mind in your home."

CHAPTER SIXTEEN

T-minus 06:12:28:45

The shocked expression on Andrea's face clearly told Kenner she had hit her mark. She'd been after her all day, and Kenner couldn't resist pulling her chain. Yanking it was more appropriate. She wasn't going to let Andrea bully or intimidate her. Far from it. She'd dealt with power-hungry, insecure people before, and Andrea was just one more. She knew how to handle her, and she just had. But Susie had to work tonight, and now she had nowhere to go. But no way in hell would she let Andrea know that little fact.

This wasn't the first time someone had assumed she was having sex. Sure, she'd slept with a lot of women. So what? They were willing, and Kenner had made it clear what it was and what it wasn't. It was the mutual enjoyment of each other, and it was not the beginning of a relationship of any kind. Having sex with a woman was no different than having dinner together or going to see a movie. If they both wanted to do it, why not?

She didn't understand women who had to be emotionally involved or had to "feel something" for the woman before they could have sex. Sex was a physical act, nothing more. What did emotion have to do with it? If anyone started to get serious or wanted exclusivity, Kenner calmly explained the facts of her life and ended their liaison. It had only gotten sticky once, and she'd had to practically pry the woman off her to get out the door. Needless to say, that one experience had been scary, and she didn't plan to ever let it happen again.

But what was she going to do about tonight? Where in the hell would she sleep? She remembered seeing a cot in the women's locker room yesterday, and her first thought had been that it was the perfect place for a quickie. She'd never thought she'd actually sleep on it. But she'd spent the night in worse places, and the expression on Andrea's face would make it worth it.

Unfortunately the cot was as lumpy as it looked, and Kenner tossed and turned most of the night. She finally gave up and went to the cafeteria around five fifteen. Surprisingly several people were there, and the smell of bacon and fresh coffee made her stomach growl. She picked up a tray and placed her order.

"Hey, stranger."

Kenner opened her eyes and saw Susie standing in front of her table. She had closed them for just a minute and wondered if she'd fallen asleep. She also wondered if her mouth had been hanging open and if she was drooling. "Hey, yourself," she replied, motioning for Susie to join her. She was surprised when the woman sat beside her and not across from her.

"Sorry I couldn't make it last night," Susie said, frowning. "If I'd had any idea you'd call, I wouldn't have volunteered to work."

Kenner shook her head. "It's okay. It was last minute, and I certainly didn't expect you to change your plans."

Susie's smile turned sexy and her eyes darkened. "I would have if it had been anything else."

Tingling started between Kenner's legs, and her brain flashed to the cot. But her back said otherwise. "We'll have to make it another time," she said. Like the instant she checked into a hotel. Susie had told her she had a roommate, and between that and her bunking arrangements at Andrea's, this hook-up was just a little more challenging than usual. But if Susie was half as good as she looked, it would be worth it.

"You seem a little tired," Susie said. "Somebody keep you up last night?" she asked, pouting a little.

That was a warning flag in Kenner's book, and she spoke carefully. "As a matter of fact, yes," she said evasively. Let Susie draw her own conclusions. It also put some distance between them if she was thinking of getting too chummy.

Susie scooted closer and put her hand on Kenner's leg, the other around the back of her chair. Kenner thought she might lick her neck. Instead she whispered, "I hope I didn't miss my chance." Her voice had dropped to a baby-doll tone.

That was warning number two, and it was time for Kenner to leave. But before she had a chance to say anything, a loud crash echoed in the near-empty room. Both she and Susie looked up to see Andrea across the way, her tray and its contents on the floor in front of her. Kenner spotted Andrea's panicked expression before she quickly knelt to pick up her mess. Kenner used the distraction as an opportunity to excuse herself, slide her chair away from Susie, and leave her table.

"Need some help?" Kenner asked, approaching Andrea.

"No, I've got it, thanks," Andrea said quickly, her once-pale face now flushed.

Kenner ignored her and knelt to pick up a container of yogurt. Luckily it hadn't exploded when it hit the floor.

Andrea reached it first and snapped, "I said I've got this."

Kenner felt the sting of Andrea's tone. "Jesus. I was just being polite."

"Well, I don't think Susie would think it polite for you to run to my rescue after spending the night with her."

Andrea stood and Kenner did as well. Kenner looked into Andrea's eyes, which appeared angry and hurt. An odd combination for someone who had told her very clearly to get lost.

Andrea broke eye contact first. Kenner's body responded as Andrea stared at her from head to toe. Did her eyes linger a little longer on her chest? Could Andrea see her tight nipples? Could she sense her arousal that hit her the instant Andrea's eyes moved over her? Holy shit.

"You may not care about how you look, but get yourself cleaned up before you come into my control room."

Kenner couldn't miss the personalization Andrea put on the words control room. She was regaining the upper hand and establishing who was on top this time. Holy fuck. The thought of Andrea on top of her almost made her knees buckle.

"I mean it, Kenner. Either make yourself presentable or don't come in."

"Or what?" Kenner shot back, her eyes blazing.

"Don't push me, Kenner," Andrea said, her teeth clenched so tight she thought they'd break.

"Or what?" Kenner repeated. "What are you going to do, send me to my room? Oh yeah, that's right. I don't have a room because your people fucked up." Kenner pointed at her before continuing. "Fire me? You won't and you know it. But if you change your mind, please do, because I was having a lot more fun and had a lot less of this bullshit to deal with where I was."

Kenner studied her for a few seconds longer before brushing past her and walking out the door.

CHAPTER SEVENTEEN

T-minus 05:43:08:55

Andrea felt her control returning. She fell back on what she knew was best—take command and take control of a horrible situation. At least it was horrible for her. When she had seen Kenner and Susie in their cozy post-coital position, her mind had gone blank, and when Susie had started sucking on Kenner's ear, she'd dropped her tray.

Somehow she was able to maintain some dignity as she walked out of the dining room. The only good thing was that, other than the two lovebirds, only a few people had witnessed her embarrassment. She held her head high and identified each step in her head as she left the scene. Left, right, left, right; the familiar cadence sang in her head. She needed to force herself in order to keep putting one foot in front of the other to get to her office, where she could then collapse in private.

She successfully made it, and once the door was locked, she leaned back against it and slid to the floor. Her hands were shaking, and she was dizzy and having trouble catching her breath. Jesus, what was wrong with her?

Andrea didn't know how long she sat there, but when noise in the hall caught her attention, she stood. She smoothed her pants, re-tucked her shirt, and positioned her belt buckle directly in the center of her stomach. She wiped her face with both hands and unlocked the door, ready to face another day.

Andrea didn't know whether she was relieved or disappointed when Kenner was in attendance at the morning briefing. Her hair was damp and she was wearing a teal-colored polo shirt with NASA embroidered over her left breast. The shirt was similar to the one Andrea had bought in the gift shop for her dad last Christmas, but it certainly fit him differently than it did her.

Her eyes kept straying to Kenner, and unlike yesterday's fiasco of a meeting, Andrea forced herself to concentrate on everything that was said. She took copious notes, referring to them often when she asked for clarification or when the team members backtracked to rehash the status of something. Every time Kenner spoke, Andrea could have sworn her heart skipped a couple of beats, and then her blood simmered with anger because her body had betrayed her. She didn't want anything to do with Kenner. She didn't care who she had sex with. All she cared about was turning this failing mission into a success.

When no one was looking at her, Andrea was looking at Kenner. She had a red mark on her neck, but from this distance Andrea couldn't tell if it was a hickey or just a red mark of some kind. Her stomach churned at the thought of what Kenner had been doing and what Susie had been doing to Kenner for her to get that hickey.

When the meeting was over she stood, and everyone filed out of the room. Andrea breathed a sigh of relief when Kenner was one of them. Unfortunately, that relief didn't last long because Barry was waiting for her on the other side of the door.

"See you a minute, Andrea."

"Of course," she said, stepping back into the room. As Barry shut the door behind them her brain went into overdrive. What did he want to talk about? She was due to brief him after this meeting. Everyone was working hard together to solve this problem. Everyone except Kenner, of course. Andrea didn't sit down in the chair she'd recently vacated, preferring to stand. If Barry was going to come down on her about something, she didn't want to be sitting while he stood over her pointing his finger. Staying on her feet was a subtle gesture, but it gave her the confidence she needed.

"What's up?" she asked, showing Barry she wasn't going to shy away from any conversation with him

Barry looked at her, hard. Andrea kept telling herself, don't move, maintain eye contact.

"How is Kenner Hutchings working out?"

Shit, Andrea thought. This was about Kenner? Why did everything have to be about Kenner? "She's working well with the team. She's starting to grasp the big picture and how all of the systems relate to each other. She asks good questions."

"But is she contributing?"

"She's helped some of the areas look at things differently. Like I said, she's asking the right questions and getting everyone to rethink, to not just assume they know the answer."

"But is she solving this problem?" Barry asked. He finally sat down.

Andrea followed him, thankful that in addition to controlling how she answered Barry's questions, she didn't need to continue to worry that her shaking legs wouldn't hold her up much longer. "If we had a solution, Barry, I would have let you know. First thing."

"We're running out of time, Andrea."

"I'm aware of that," she replied. The look on Barry's face told her just how sharp her tone was. 'We're getting there, Barry. We're making progress. Not only are we ruling things out, but we're almost to the point that we can start zeroing in and focusing on key areas. Kenner is a big part of that process."

"We're paying through the nose for her, Andrea. I need to see results."

This statement infuriated Andrea. She understood his position. He was management, so his concern was the budget, the schedule, the public relations. She, however, was worried about the life and death of the crew members entrusted to her care. She didn't give a shit how much it cost to get them home safely. Her job was to do it.

She tempered her anger when she said, "I understand that, Barry. I can't speak to that point, but I can understand how someone with Kenner's skill and experience and reputation would not come for free. She's worth every penny."

Andrea was surprised at her own statement. Wasn't it just yesterday she'd accused Kenner of being lazy because she was shooting hoops on the basketball court? And wasn't it the day before that she did the same thing because Kenner had her feet on the console?

"I've done a little digging on Miss Hutchings."

Andrea's breakfast, what little she'd been able to eat after this morning's humiliation, started to churn.

Barry looked to his left, then right, as if checking to see that no one could overhear them. God, now what?

"She's a lesbian," Barry said, his teeth clenched with barely concealed disgust.

Andrea choked back a laugh of disbelief. Had he actually said that? I need to be very careful here, she thought. "And?"

"And? Is that all you have to say, 'And'?" Barry mimicked her word.

"That doesn't matter."

"It doesn't?"

Jesus, was he going to repeat everything she said? "No, it doesn't."

"Why not?"

"Because she's not here to have sex with someone to get the magic key that will start the engines."

The look on Barry's face told her she might have overstepped her bounds far. She wasn't so far down the path that she couldn't stop and backtrack, but damn it, she didn't want to.

"Barry, you said it yourself. We're paying for her brain and her skills and her deductive reasoning. Good God, she looked at the schematics for the payload doors one time and immediately understood everything about them. She spent two hours with both Gyro and Propulsion, and she completely understands how they relate to each other. That's what we're paying her for. That's what we need her to do. And whether she's a lesbian or straight or a nun, I don't care. This mission doesn't care, the seven astronauts don't care. Because it doesn't matter." Her voice got stronger as she continued her argument.

"If someone thinks that it does matter, you need to set them straight, Barry. You do," she said, pointing at him and knowing that he was the one who needed to be set straight. But she didn't tell him that. "People respect you, Barry. They listen to you, take your lead, and you need to step above this. Everyone will see your stance, and they will do the same. If you make it a big deal, it will become one. If you don't..." She let her voice fall away to let Barry reach his own conclusion. "So if you'll excuse me," she said brazenly before he could counter her statement with an argument of his own. "I need to get back to the control room.

She hesitated for a few moments, giving him the opportunity to keep her there if he wanted to say anything else. When he didn't, she stood. "I know you'll do the right thing, Barry. I'll talk to you later." She exited the conference room, leaving the door open behind her.

This time when she walked down the hall, her legs were a little weak and her hands were shaking from anger. She hadn't realized that her boss thought this way, but it was clear that he did. She breathed a sigh of relief that she had kept her private life private. She wasn't in the closet but also didn't comment on things that were nobody's business. She talked about her weekend plans, just like everyone else did. Everyone knew she was single, and they also knew she was totally committed to her work. What they thought of that, she didn't care. All she did care about was how they thought of her as a leader.

She was absolutely safe from any speculation. She hadn't heard any gossip going around about her. She knew enough people that would tell her. But Barry thinking that Kenner was not qualified to do this job just because of who she had sex with was abhorrent. She would need to be very careful with her interactions with Kenner in the future.

Andrea walked into the control room, and nobody lifted their head to see who had come in. Her team members were dedicated. They had a job to do and they were doing it. She made her way through the room, stopping for a few minutes at each station. She asked a few questions and answered others but generally was just getting the feel of what was going on.

As she approached Kenner's workstation she contemplated passing by it and moving on to the next one. What would that say to everyone? That Kenner didn't matter? That she was just a showpiece? Not adding any value? What would that say to Kenner? That she was afraid of her? Afraid of what Kenner might say? What she'd insinuate? Afraid to be around her, to talk to her? Andrea stepped forward and put aside everything personal about this situation and pulled out her professionalism. She stopped just behind Kenner's left shoulder.

Kenner knew Andrea was behind her. Somehow she always knew when Andrea was around. Of course people were always aware when bad news was coming. And Andrea was definitely bad news. "Look, if you're going to rag on me, or bitch at me, or criticize me, can we do it later? I'm working on something right now."

Kenner didn't care how she sounded. She really didn't. She'd decided she was here for one thing and one thing only. Get this job done, add another bullet to her resumé, take her paycheck to the bank, and move on. She could do that, she'd done it before. This was like high school and college. You do what you need to do. You keep your eyes and ears open, your mouth shut, your head down, and do your work.

Surprisingly, Andrea didn't say anything, and it wasn't long before she moved on to the station to her left. Kenner was relieved they weren't going to have another verbal sparring match, because quite frankly she didn't know how much more she could take. No one had ever set her off like Andrea did. She never allowed anyone to have that much power over her because that meant they got under her skin. And nobody got under her skin. That meant she cared. And that meant that person had the power to hurt her, and no one would ever hurt her like Eva had.

She had planned to spend the rest of her life with Eva Compton. They'd met when Kenner was in grad school at MIT. Kenner had just turned twenty, and Eva worked as a waitress on the night shift at the coffee shop Kenner frequented during her many bouts with insomnia. Kenner didn't have many friends, if any, really. Even at that stage of her education she was still the odd one in class, only this time not just as still the smartest but the youngest, and the animosity was ferocious. Whereas in grade school and high school the traditional competition had revolved around boy-girl relationships, the mocking of Kenner had centered on her freakish brain and her butch dress and behavior. In college and even grad school, everyone was supposed to be more mature, at least theoretically, so the animosity was far more subtle. Everyone was vying to be the top of their class and get the premier job offer, which came with big bucks. Most didn't care who they stepped on, or over, or even crushed to get there. And Kenner was the prime target.

Their conversations had started out innocent enough, Eva sitting across from Kenner when the coffee shop wasn't busy. Fortunately, or what Kenner came to realize later, unfortunately that was almost every night. The topics had begun innocuously enough: the weather, movies, funny stories about Eva's customers and Kenner's classmates. But when their conversations moved from the diner to a real restaurant, to Kenner's living room and ultimately her bed, their communication became very nonverbal. Eva was the first person who had looked at her and recognized her for who she was. She wasn't interested in exploiting Kenner's brain for her own personal gain, amusement, or benefit. Or at least Kenner had thought so. No, she'd believed so. Until Eva ran off with a traveling salesman.

At first Kenner thought Stan, Eva's boss, was joking when he told her. A traveling salesman? How clichéd was that? But after weeks of silence to her voice messages and texts, Kenner finally accepted the fact that Eva had left.

She was devastated, to say the least, because she had pretty much kept to herself during most of her turbulent adolescent years. Eva had been her first, and as such Kenner had fallen hard. Very hard. She had opened herself up to Eva, spilling her hopes and dream and fears. She had laughed, cried, hidden, and explored life with her. But in the end, it had all come crumbling down on and around her head. She wasn't interested in experiencing that trauma again and kept her subsequent relationships superficial.

Kenner thought about the last twelve hours. How had her situation gone from a simple question about her hotel, to sleeping on a fucking cot in the locker room, to getting reamed out by Andrea because of the false impression she had about her and Susie? Would they ever be able to have a decent, civilized conversation? Or even a professional one? Their acquaintance had barely started out that way and had gone drastically downhill from there.

Kenner forced her attention back to the screen in front of her and concentrated on the numbers. She pulled up a schematic on her second screen, then bent closer and picked up her pencil and started jotting furiously. She was on to something. She wasn't certain what exactly, but it was something. A piece of the puzzle had fallen into place, and she grabbed at it like a drowning man grabbing a lifeline.

The clicking of fingers on keyboards and constant subdued conversation around her disappeared, and her focus became razor sharp on the data in front of her. She filled up page after page with notes, jotting down theories based on what she'd discovered. She fleshed each one out, outlining her thoughts and then zeroing in on specific steps. She didn't realize how long she'd been working until a sheet of paper slid in front of her. Irritated at the interruption, she glanced at it and saw the logo of a local hotel along with the words *reservation confirmation* and her name. After writing a few more notes on the pad, she put her pencil down and picked up the paper.

Her first glance proved correct. It confirmed that she had a room at a hotel she'd seen on one of the streets they'd passed while driving to and from Andrea's house. She was in a suite with a king-size bed and breakfast, and a rental car was waiting for her when she checked in.

She looked around, expecting to see Andrea hovering nearby with a smile on her face, relieved to be losing her houseguest. "Where's the boss?" she asked the middle-aged man with a crew cut and forty extra pounds to her left.

"I don't know," he mumbled.

When no further conversation or possible location of Andrea was forthcoming, Kenner stood up and stretched, the bones in her back popping. She'd been hunched over her desk all day, and the growling of her stomach told her she'd missed lunch. It was ten minutes after seven, and she was more than ready for dinner. She could run down to the cafeteria and grab something, but she didn't want to keep Andrea waiting. It would probably piss her off, and Kenner weighed that option for a few seconds before deciding against it. Instead she hit the vending machine down the hall, slid her card through the reader, and selected a package of cinnamon Pop Tarts and a Cherry Coke.

When she turned the fourth corner to get back to the control room, she saw Andrea swiping her badge to enter. She hurried to catch up. "Hey, Andrea."

The security guard stood, blocking the doorway. "No tailgating," she said, a frown stretched across her forehead.

"What?" Kenner was confused.

"Tailgate. That's what it's called when you follow someone into a secured area without badging in yourself," Andrea said.

"But the door is already open."

"It's not a matter of opening the door but personnel accountability." Andrea's tone was one of annoyance, like she was explaining something very simple. "This is a highly secured facility," she said, like Kenner was an idiot. "And absolute accountability for every person in this building and where they are authorized to enter is a requirement."

"So big brother follows us everywhere," Kenner said, more than a little sarcastic.

"For security reasons."

Andrea didn't move, and this conversation was verging on the ridiculous. Because of that, and the fact that the security butch was looking at her suspiciously, Kenner said, "Oh, for God's sake," and swiped her badge next to the door. Andrea stepped into the room, and the blinking green light on the card reader was Kenner's reward for following orders.

"Andrea," Kenner said again.

Andrea turned around, an annoyed look on her face.

"The hotel room."

"What?"

"My hotel room. You gave me the paper with the reservation information."

"Oh, yes," she said. And that was all she said. God, getting any information out of her was like pulling the sword from a stone.

"I'm ready whenever you are."

"All right. Give me ten minutes to finish up and we'll leave."

Exactly ten minutes later they were walking down the hall toward the security doors. Kenner finally opened her soda, the hissing sound of the pressure being released drawing Andrea's attention.

"What?" Kenner asked, taking a swallow of her Coke.

"Is that a snack or dinner?" Andrea asked, pushing open the double doors in front of them.

"Yep," Kenner answered, just before taking a bite of the Pop Tart. She didn't say anything else. She wasn't in the mood for a fight or a dressing down about her dietary habits from the Miss-Perfect Andrea Finley. She was an hour from freedom, and it tasted much better than the snack she held. She didn't want her mood spoiled so she just kept her mouth shut except to keep eating. She knew Andrea was expecting her to say something else, but she could wait. She could wait all she wanted.

It wasn't until they got into the car that Andrea asked, "Are you going to give me the silent treatment for the rest of the time you're here?"

So much for her good mood and not saying anything. "What is with you, Andrea? I mean, really. You're less than an hour away from getting rid of me, and you still have to snip and snipe at me? But unlike you, I don't want another confrontation. I want to check into my hotel, take a shower, change my clothes, find something decent to eat, and watch the baseball game."

Andrea chuckled and shook her head. Against Kenner's better judgment she asked, "What is it now?"

"That's all you're going to do? I would have thought Susie would have been on your doorstep."

"Well, you're mistaken again, Andrea. Wait a minute," Kenner said, turning to look at her. She was in profile, and Kenner tried not to notice that she had a perfect nose. "Is that what pisses you off so much about me? The fact that you're wrong so many times?" Andrea glanced over at her. "Keep your eyes on the road," Kenner demanded. "For God's sake, it's bumper-to-bumper traffic." Andrea looked back at the cars in front of her and had to swerve to miss the one that had stopped in front of her due to the traffic.

"What do you mean?"

"What do I mean?" Kenner was dumbfounded. "I mean everything you thought you knew about me about me was wrong. Everything you've assumed about me is just the opposite. You're probably never wrong, or at least no one has had the guts to tell you when you are. You probably think things through to the nth degree, so you're certain about everything."

"That's not true." Andrea sounded like a petulant child.

"Yes, Andrea, it is. You don't approve of anything I do. You don't think I'm dressed appropriately, you don't like the way I sit, you don't like the way I work. You don't like the way I relax. You don't like anything about me. Everything about me is like nails on a chalkboard to you. And you can't handle it."

"I don't know what you're talking about," Andrea said defensively.

Kenner held up her hand. "I'm not going to have this argument with you. Just get me to my hotel and we'll be done with each other."

"What about your suitcase?"

"No way am I spending a minute more with you in this car than I have to. Just bring it in tomorrow." The more Kenner thought about this entire conversation the angrier she got.

They sat in silence for the rest of the drive, Andrea looking out the windshield and Kenner the passenger window. Maybe it was because of the close quarters they were in, but the tension between them was as thick as fog on a San Francisco morning.

Kenner had never been a situation like this. She'd been in difficult, contentious situations, but never in a business setting. Especially when the lives of seven people were at stake, as Andrea kept reminding her. Like she could forget.

It's funny, she thought. Andrea's image and what she prided herself on was her utmost professionalism, but when it came to dealing with her hired expert, it appeared to fall apart. If Andrea didn't get it together pretty soon and lay off her, Kenner didn't know if she could be responsible for her actions. That was one thing she definitely didn't want to think about tonight.

Andrea pulled into the circle drive of hotel, and before the valet could reach her door handle, Kenner had leapt out of the car and slammed the door behind her.

CHAPTER EIGHTEEN

T-minus 05:27:49:02

Andrea was exhausted by the time she got home. The stress of the past few weeks, particularly the last few days with Kenner, had taken more out of her than she expected. She changed out of her work clothes and into a pair of comfortable jeans and soft T-shirt. She knew she should eat something, but she wasn't really hungry. Instead she tossed a couple of cubes of ice in a tumbler and poured two fingers of whiskey. She added another splash for good measure and walked out onto her back patio.

She loved being outside, but the bugs and mosquitos in Clear Lake made it next to impossible to enjoy. So like many of her neighbors she'd constructed a large screened-in room that covered her entire patio, her pool, and almost all of her backyard. It was the only way she could enjoy a swim in the evenings after work to unwind. She thought about stripping and diving into the clear water, but her mind was jumbled and her drink tasted far too good. That and she would probably hit her head when making a turn in the water and drown.

Andrea glanced at her watch. It was close to eleven. She had a briefcase full of work and needed to pack Kenner's things to take to the office in the morning. She couldn't help but think about Kenner. For God's sake, she hadn't been able to do anything but think about Kenner since the day she'd stepped into that conference room—what was it, only three days ago. Holy crap. She'd never had anyone cause such turmoil in her life in such a short time.

Whenever Kenner was around, Andrea couldn't think straight, her emotions getting the better of her. She'd never felt like this toward anyone. She was always on edge around her and never knew what to expect. Her calm, sedate, predictable life was anything but, and she wasn't certain how to fix it. Kenner was going to be here until they solved this problem, whether she liked it or not. But Andrea knew that once she put her mind to it, she'd gain control of her life again. The tension between them, a hum, a charge she'd never experienced, of course made things more complicated and confusing. It had been unnerving her.

Finally feeling a little more relaxed than when she got home, Andrea debated whether to have another drink or just head off to bed. She was leaning toward bed when she remembered that she had to pack Kenner's things. She could either do it now or in the morning. Deciding she needed to rid herself of Kenner in her house, she went to the guest room, stopping first in the kitchen to refill her glass with another hefty splash of liquor.

Andrea cautiously entered the room where Kenner had spent the last two nights. The bed was perfectly made, the throw pillows in the exact spot she would have placed them. The top of the dresser was empty, and the room actually looked like no one was staying there. She opened the closet door and saw Kenner's red duffle bag lying neatly in the corner. No clothes were on the hangers so she pulled the duffle out and laid it on the bed. She moved to the dresser, opening each drawer and, like the closet, finding each one empty. Obviously Kenner hadn't unpacked, probably anticipating she'd be here only one night so why bother. The bathroom was exactly the same as the closet and dresser, with the exception of the midnight-blue towel hanging slightly askew over the towel bar. That was the only indication that anyone had used this room, and Andrea admitted she was completely surprised. She'd expected clothes to be strewn everywhere, toiletries all over the counter, and the towel in a damp, musty heap on the floor. Why wouldn't she expect this, given Kenner's lackadaisical attitude?

She slid open the shower door, intending to throw away the bar of soap Kenner had used, when an image of Kenner standing inside with water sliding over her naked body stopped her. A rush of heat started in the pit of her stomach and quickly traveled through every vein and artery in her body. She staggered under the effect, stepping back to lean against the counter. Her eyes stayed frozen on the glass of the shower door and the image behind it. Her brain told her Kenner wasn't there, but her body was telling her otherwise.

She saw Kenner's soapy hand travel up and down her arms, across her shoulders and down her chest to cup her breasts. Andrea's mouth went dry. When Kenner's hands slid across her stomach and disappeared between her legs, Andrea couldn't stop the moan she released. The sound broke through her fantasy and made her abruptly face the reality that not only was the shower empty, but it was also absolutely spotless.

Andrea's hands were shaking as she grabbed the towel and washcloth. She crossed through the bathroom and tossed the towels onto the bed. She'd deal with them tomorrow. Her legs were shaking as she picked up Kenner's duffle. She decided to leave it outside in the hallway so she wouldn't' forget it in the morning. "Like I could forget anything about Kenner," she said to the empty room. Changing her mind, she dropped the duffle on the floor, tossed the pillows and comforter onto the chair beside the bed, and started to strip the bed. Might as well put all this in the wash tonight and get it over with, she thought.

She tugged at the sheets, pulling the edges toward the center. And when she reached for the pillow, the unmistakable scent of Kenner drifted off the cotton, and heat like a bolt of lightning shot through her all the way to her toes. *Oh my God, this smells like Kenner.* Andrea had never noticed Kenner wearing any perfume or cologne, but this was definitely her. Without thinking, she brought the pillow closer to her face and closed her eyes. As the soft fabric brushed against her cheek, she inhaled deeply.

Images of Kenner flashed through her mind. The first time she saw her in the conference room, the wide-eyed wonder when she took her on a tour of the station, the look of complete relaxation as she sat at her workstation, and her graceful athleticism as she'd moved on the basketball court yesterday.

Her knees suddenly went weak, and Andrea turned and sat down on the bed as more images danced behind her eyelids. The sound of her laughter at a joke one of her coworkers told. The way her face lit up when she talked about anything. The sincerity of her smile. The twinkle in her eyes, the heat in her look, the desire behind those big green eyes that she didn't even bother to mask.

"Oh, my God," Andrea said, falling back to lie on the bed. "What in the hell is going on?" she asked herself after taking the pillow away from her face. Her mind was in chaos, which wasn't at all like her. She hadn't thought clearly in days. She closed her eyes again and put her forearm on her forehead, trying desperately to regain her equilibrium. But instead of settling down, she envisioned Kenner hovering above her. The passion and desire on her face took Andrea's breath away. When Kenner lowered her head to kiss her, Andrea started to reach up to push her away. Instead, though, she gave up and lost herself in the fantasy.

Kenner's kisses were alternately sweet, then demanding. They were soft like a butterfly's wings caressing her lips, then hard, her tongue plunging inside in domination. She kissed Andrea's eyelids, her cheeks, and the tip of her nose. She nipped her bottom lip, then lightly sucked until the sting subsided. She nibbled at her earlobe and slid her tongue down the side of her neck, returning eagerly to her mouth.

Her touch was equally varied. One minute it was so light it almost tickled and the next firm as if memorizing the texture of every inch of her. Andrea arched into Kenner's touch, seeking more contact to obtain release. Her pulse raced through her veins, roared in her ears, and heated her skin. Andrea slid her hands into Kenner's hair and pulled her mouth where she wanted it. Unfortunately her clothes were in the way, and she let go long enough to pull her shirt over her head before directing Kenner to her breasts. She moaned when Kenner lightly bit down on one nipple. The sensation of Kenner's teeth through her lace bra sent a bolt of pleasure directly between her legs, and Andrea pulled her even closer.

When Kenner transferred her attention to Andrea's other breast, she wrapped her leg around the back of Kenner's thigh, effectively trapping her tight against her throbbing clit.

"God, yes," Andrea said unabashed at her inability to contain her pleasure. Just the feel of Kenner's mouth on her breasts had her teetering toward orgasm. Her breath was coming fast and her entire body was on fire. She felt Kenner's fingers working the zipper on her jeans, and she lifted her hips when Kenner slid them down her hips. When Kenner's hands come back to her skin, Andrea shimmied out of her jeans and kicked them off.

Kenner's shirt was bunched in her hands, and Andrea dragged it and her undershirt over Kenner's head and tossed them to the floor also. Kenner's skin was hot under her fingers, and Andrea ran her hands liberally up and down her smooth back. She felt Kenner's muscles tense as she touched her. There was still one barrier between them.

"I need to feel you against me," she said, her breath coming in gasps.

Kenner lifted her head and quickly popped the front clasp, dispensing her bra in the general direction of all their other clothes. When Kenner didn't immediately move Andrea opened her eyes. Kenner was looking directly at her, her dark eyes smoldering with desire. Kenner held their gaze as she slowly lowered her body back onto hers. Andrea gasped when their nipples touched under Kenner's perfect descent.

Andrea tried to pull Kenner completely against her, but Kenner resisted.

"Wait," Kenner whispered, her voice husky.

Andrea's breath caught in her throat as Kenner shifted her hips and increased the pressure on her clit. Back and forth she moved, slowly and deliberately, their nipples flicking against each other with each downward move. Andrea dug what few fingernails she had into Kenner's back as she slowly climbed to orgasm.

She was in agony, ecstasy, and everything in between as Kenner moved against her. One arm was braced above her head for leverage, her other hand gripping her hip. Kenner's eyes still had not let her go, and Andrea felt herself falling. She started to close her eyes but Kenner said, "Open your eyes, Andrea."

Andrea heard her name called somewhere in the haze of pleasure and did as she was told. Kenner's eyes were burning, deep pools of desire she could easily drown in.

"I want to see your eyes the first time I make you come."

Andrea lost her breath at the power of those few words. No one had ever said them to her, and she wasn't sure she could grant Kenner's wish. She'd had sex with numerous women who had come back for more, but she was still a bit shy about the actual act. She could be naked in front of them, have their mouths on her in those perfect places, but she could never look them in the eye. That was almost too personal, too intimate. Like there could be anything more intimate than sharing your body with another.

But there was something absolutely overpowering about Kenner, and Andrea could not deny her. It took both a physical and emotional effort to lift her eyelids, and the instant their eyes locked she came.

Her orgasm started at the tip of her toes and blew out the top of her head. She arched against Kenner, lifting her legs for more firm contact. Kenner pushed her pubic bone into her, and Andrea locked her legs around her hips. Shudder after agonizing shudder racked her body, each more unbearable in pleasure than the one before. She felt like she was shattering like a crystal glass under the tone of a perfect soprano, and she didn't know if she would survive. She wasn't sure she wanted to, because nothing and no other woman making love to her could ever equal this.

Slowly the world began to regain focus and Andrea could no longer keep her eyes open. She was spent. Completely, entirely spent. Kenner taking her to orgasm had consumed her and her body, though still tingling, felt like it didn't belong to her. The messages from her brain telling her legs to unclench weren't going through. The normal rhythm of her breathing had not yet returned an she wasn't sure she could even remember her name.

Her world turned upside down when Kenner rolled them both and Andrea found herself on top of Kenner. Using her arms she pushed up into a sitting position opening her legs, to straddle Kenner's stomach. She still had her panties on but the wetness between her legs and soaked through the thin material. Kenner's eyes shot to that area and a new wave of heat slipped from her body.

"You're beautiful," Kenner said, her voice full of desire. Her hands followed her eyes as they traveled slowly up and down Andrea's torso, reigniting the flame between her legs. "You are so beautiful," Kenner said as she slipped her fingers under the edge of her dark-blue panties.

Andrea inhaled in response to the instant sensation of pleasure. She shifted to try to escape the pull of another orgasm, but Kenner held her firm. With incredible patience, Kenner moved past the thin lace edge and lightly touched her lips. Andrea's body knew what she wanted and surged into the exploring fingers, urging them closer.

"Please," Andrea said, without realizing the word came out of her mouth. Her eyes went to Kenner's and her mouth went dry and her breath hitched. Kenner's eyes were blazing, and Andrea had never seen anything so mesmerizing.

"Please what?" Kenner asked, her finger skidding over her clit.

Andrea was only capable of a moan. She arched back, her hands on the top of Kenner's thighs for support.

"Tell me what you want, Andrea."

Kenner's voice was thick with desire, and the sound of her name almost took Andrea over the edge.

"Tell me. Say it." Kenner's voice was more demanding now, causing Andrea to open her eyes and look at her. "Tell me, Andrea. Tell me what you want."

Andrea couldn't stop the words from tumbling out of her mouth. Words that had never crossed her lips. Words she had never uttered to anyone, even under the anonymity of the black night.

"Touch me."

Chapter Nineteen

T-minus 05:16:41:38

Andrea woke, and for a moment she panicked. Her arms and legs were bound, and she didn't immediately recognize where she was. Slowly it dawned on her that she was in the guest bed, Kenner's bed, the sheets wrapped around her like a cocoon. "Oh, God," she said, remembering the events of the night before.

She had deliberately picked a fight with Kenner on the way home, and when Kenner had demanded to be let off at her hotel, Andrea had readily complied. She'd had a drink—no, wait, two drinks—and somehow ended up in this bed. And her dreams. Dear God, she'd dreamed of having sex with Kenner all night.

First it was in this very bed, soft and sweet. Andrea usually could remember only vague aspects of her dreams, but she recalled every touch of Kenner's body on hers. The sound of Kenner's voice whispering to her, "Tell me," was so clear she turned her head to make sure she really wasn't there. She remembered how splashing in the pool had turned from lighthearted fun to something much more serious. Another time she was wrapped in Kenner's strong arms rolling in the sand, which was probably how she'd ended up almost mummified in her four-hundred-thread-count sheets. Just thinking about her dreams made her clit throb, and she involuntarily squeezed her legs together. That was a mistake, and she groaned as she forced herself up and out of the bed.

Andrea looked at herself in her bathroom mirror as she waited for the shower water to heat. "Oh, my God," she said to her reflection in the large mirror above the sink. Her hair was disheveled, she had circles under her eyes, but her face was flushed. She was a wreck, and after glancing at the clock she realized she didn't have much time to pull herself together.

Freshly showered, she carefully pulled on her clothes. After the last twenty-four hours she needed some extra self-assurance and donned her "don't fuck with me" suit. It was black with thin, white pinstripes, its matching jacket featuring a mandarin collar. Her gray shirt was the perfect accent, as were her patent-leather loafers and belt, so she was ready to face the day…and Kenner.

Andrea sat in her car debating whether to take Kenner's duffle inside or leave it here for her to pick up later. Then she realized that if she took it in, people would ask questions, and that was the last thing she needed. She got out of the car and slammed the door a little harder than necessary, frustrated over her lack of sleep and then sitting in her car for five minutes debating something as stupid as a duffle bag. She scanned the parking lot with as much casualness as she could without drawing attention to the fact that she was, in fact, looking for someone. She was looking for Kenner, and when she realized she didn't even know what kind of rental car she had, Andrea was even angrier at herself. She practically stomped through the parking lot, bulldozed her way through security, and didn't say a word to anyone she passed through the hallways to the elevator.

She was alone in the elevator, the doors closing, when a hand shot between them, activating the sensor to reopen them. Kenner dashed in, breathless, obviously having run to catch the elevator.

"Sorry, thanks," Kenner said as she hustled into the car. She stopped, suddenly noticing Andrea for the first time.

The picture of a breathless, naked Kenner in her dream swam into focus. The image was so overpowering Andrea had to take a step back and grab the handrail. The air in the small car suddenly wasn't sufficient, and Andrea fought to keep her breathing steady. Her body was screaming something unfamiliar, and her head started spinning. Visions of Kenner in her bed below her, on top of her, inside her were all she could see.

Andrea knew where she was but had no idea what was happening to her. The sensation that had taken over her body was foreign to her, and she struggled to pull herself back to the here and now before she completely humiliated herself here in this elevator.

"Andrea?"

Kenner's voice penetrated her flashback. "I'm sorry, what?" Andrea somehow managed to say.

"I asked if you were all right. Your face is flushed, and it looked like you went somewhere else for a minute."

"I'm fine," she replied, hurriedly dragging her eyes from Kenner's face to focus on the ascending numbers above the door. Andrea didn't trust herself to know what was real or fantasy, and before she made a fool out of herself she needed to get out of this elevator, and she needed to get out right now.

The doors opened on the floor below hers, and before two men entered the elevator she hurried off, not looking behind her. She didn't want to see the confused or concerned look on Kenner's face. She hurried up the stairs to her floor.

Andrea dropped her keys on the floor in front of her office door. Her hand were still shaking, and she cursed that, as she bent to pick them up, her forehead hit the door knob. She took a deep breath and tried again, this time successfully opening the door. She closed it behind her, crossed to her desk, sat down, and held her head in her hands.

It was going to be a very, very long day, and she never felt like that. Usually she was so busy she'd sit down, and before she knew it, it was way past time to go home. She had thought she'd sleep better with Kenner out of her house and no longer her responsibility, but then she'd had the dreams. Not wanting to go down that memory lane again, Andrea stood up so fast her chair slid backward and bumped into the credenza behind her. She hurried out the door and to the break room down the hall. She needed a good, strong cup of coffee to get everything back on track.

Don't look for her, don't look for her, Andrea repeated to herself as she walked toward the control room. Andrea had told herself to stop thinking about Kenner and definitely not look for her the instant she entered the room. She had to focus, get her team to come up with results. Barry was breathing down her back, and the head of NASA was due on-site in two days.

When Barry had told her Richard Marconi was coming down from Washington, D.C., along with several members of the Office of Management and Budget, she'd been more than a little annoyed. That was the last thing she needed. Marconi was a U.S. Senator and chairman of the committee and probably wouldn't know the space shuttle from the Mercury capsule. Of course Andrea tried to never think about anything other than the fact that he was the head of the agency that employed her and therefore deserved her respect. But she didn't need the egotistical bastard and his purse-string cronies crowding her control room. Not when they had so much work to do. She'd have to find a way to get them in and out in record time.

She was still thinking about their guests when she showed her badge to the guard at the main control-room door. She wanted to ask if Kenner had arrived but forced herself not to. Don't look for her, don't look for her, she repeated with each step as she entered the room and the door closed behind her.

Andrea wanted to look to her right at the workstation Kenner had occupied the past few days. If she wasn't there she was usually looking over the shoulder at another station or had her feet up on her desk, or she was shooting hoops. Andrea wouldn't know if Kenner was here until the morning briefing in, she glanced at her watch, fifteen minutes.

The phone on her desk rang and she keyed her headset. "Flight Director Finley," she said, trying to anticipate who was on the other end of the line.

"Ms. Finley, this is Richard Marconi," the gravelly voice said in her ear.

"Senator Marconi, hello. How are you?"

"I'd be better if you told me those seven astronauts were on their way home." His voice sounded nothing short of irritated.

"I wish I could, sir, but we're working on it."

"When do you think you might have something, Director Finley?"

Andrea thought carefully before she spoke. This was her boss's boss, after all, and she was already on thin ice with him. "Senator Marconi, you know better than I," she said, giving him credit that wasn't due, "that we have to be very careful as we figure this out. If we rush it, have one misstep, one incorrect calculation, one number transposed, we could have a very public disaster on our hands."

"A bigger one than those astronauts starving to death or suffocating from lack of oxygen on the moon on live TV?"

Obviously her approach to get him to back off hadn't worked. "No sir, of course not. We have to bring them home, and my team will do that."

"Then what is the holdup?" he demanded.

This man couldn't be this clueless, she thought. He wouldn't know exactly, but he had to have some idea of the complexity of the hundreds of systems and millions of lines of code that were involved with getting to the moon and back. She rubbed her eyes. God, she was tired.

"Senator, we are doing the best we can. We have the brightest minds in—"

"You brought in Hutch, or Starsky, or somebody like that from some think tank?"

"Kenner Hutchings," Andrea told him. His reference to the street-wise, crime-fighting detectives in the 1970s television series was insulting to her mission and all of NASA, but she kept her mouth shut.

"Whoever," he said dismissively. "She's costing the taxpayers a fortune, who, by the way, pay your salary as well."

His threats did not intimidate her. "Senator, if you don't have anything else, I have to get back." She paused for a moment just to be polite, then said, "You'll know something as soon as we do, Senator. Thank you for calling." She hung up the phone and had an almost desperate need to wash her hands and face.

❖

Andrea stepped through the door, kicked her shoes off, and set her briefcase and keys on the counter. She didn't know why she'd opened the refrigerator door, because it didn't have anything substantial in it to eat. But she needed something, so she scrambled a couple of eggs, tossed in a handful of cheese, and dinner was served.

On her way to the table she took her phone out of her briefcase and thumbed through her personal email between bites. She'd seen too many accidents caused from texting and driving, so she eliminated any temptation by putting her phone and briefcase in the trunk. She had a note from her sister acknowledging that she was probably extremely busy but to give her a call when she had the chance. Andrea tapped on the shortcut for Beth and, while the phone rang, finished the remaining eggs on her plate.

"Hey, stranger," came the familiar voice from the speaker. "I didn't expect to hear from you for a couple of weeks."

"Yeah. Well, I actually had a minute and out of all the things on my To Do list, I pushed you to the top." That was a lie. She'd just had an unusual need to talk to someone.

"Aren't you sweet," Beth said, the sound of a baby crying in the background.

"How's Annie?" Andrea asked after hearing her new four-month-old niece.

"Just a little fussy. Paul has baby duty tonight."

"He's a keeper, Beth." Her sister's husband was definitely a jewel. There were times in Andrea's life she wanted to find a girl just like Paul, but the thought always quickly vanished. She didn't have the time or the interest to devote to cultivating a relationship like that. She never had, and she probably never would.

"How are things?" Beth asked.

Even though Beth wasn't specific, Andrea knew she was asking about the mission. "We're making progress," she answered vaguely.

"You don't sound very optimistic."

No matter how hard Andrea tried, Beth could always see right through her. Even through the magic of a wireless connection.

"Talk to me, Andi."

"I don't know…" Andrea didn't have "girl talks" so she wasn't sure how to begin.

"You don't know…how to solve it? If you're going to be able to bring them home?"

"No, I'm sure we will. I have to."

"Andi, the fate of this mission does not rest on your shoulders alone."

"Beth—"

"I know, Andi. We've been through this before, and I'm going to say it again. There is no *I* in team and there's no *U* in it either. You have, what, a hundred people working on this mission?"

"More like three or four," Andrea replied.

"Okay, you have a boatload of people working on this mission. Everyone has a part in the success, and God forbid the failure, including you. But not only you." Beth emphasized the point she'd made many times before.

"I know."

"I realize you do. But I also know you. You're not eating right, and you're probably not sleeping more than a few hours a night. You can't function that way. You are not responsible for what happened."

"Maybe not, that will be determined later, but I am responsible for fixing it."

"No, Andi. You are not responsible. Maybe you're responsible for getting it fixed. There's a difference, a big difference. You're always too hard on yourself," Beth said in a more comforting tone. "You expect too much from yourself. I know this mission is important to you. I know it's the culmination of everything you've worked for your entire life. You'd never admit that to anyone, but I'm sure of it. So tell me what's happening."

Beth always offered to listen. She got the general idea of what Andrea was talking about, but when Andrea delved into the more technical aspects, she recognized when she lost her sister. However, talking things out with someone she trusted, who in no way would pass judgment on her professional ability or her doubts and concerns, was immeasurable. It helped her think things through. She could talk out loud, think out loud, and hypothesize out loud. She could dare to verbalize wild, crazy ideas. And at the end of the conversation she usually realized what she had to do.

"We had to bring in an outsider," she said. Anyone who didn't work for NASA or one of its many hundreds of contractors was referred to as an outsider.

"And you hate that."

Andrea couldn't help but smile a little at her sister's absolutely correct statement. "Am I that much of a snob?"

"Generally no, but definitely a NASA snob."

This time Andrea actually laughed. She couldn't remember the last time she'd done that except with Kenner at the steak restaurant. "Yeah, you're probably right."

"So what does this outsider do outside of the almighty National Aeronautics and Space Administration?" If anyone other than Beth had asked such a question, it would be a barb that would fester inside Andrea. But Beth had a way of talking that made it nonthreatening.

"She comes from a think tank and is twenty-six goddamn years old. She doesn't fit in. She wears jeans, boots, and T-shirts. Her hair is about an inch long all over her head. Her boots are on the desk, her keyboard in her lap, and she plays basketball on the court downstairs in the middle of the day."

"And?" Beth prompted her.

"And she's brilliant. She's scary smart." Admittedly Andrea was in awe of that fact.

"Why are you saying that like it's a bad thing?" Beth asked carefully.

"That's the point. It shouldn't be, but I don't know why it is."

"So what is this Albert Einstein's name?"

"You know Einstein wasn't a genius."

"There you go again," Beth said, a smile in her voice. "Ruining my perception of an old guy with bad hair. Anyone who has hair like that has to be a genius. You know I always said there's a fine line between genius and insanity. What's her name?" Beth asked, reverting back to her original question.

"Kenner Hutchings."

"What kind of name is Kenner?"

"I haven't asked." It wasn't like Andrea to delve into something so personal. Hell, anything personal.

"So what's the problem?"

"I just...I've never had to work with someone like her," Andrea said, trying to explain and not doing a good job of it.

"Okay..." Andrea knew she still wasn't making any sense.

"And is there a problem with her being there?"

Boy, was there ever, Andrea admitted, but only to herself. She didn't dare go there with Beth. However, her sister had other ideas.

"What's the real problem, Andi?"

Andrea hesitated.

"Andrea?" Beth prompted her in her older-by-only-three-minutes tone.

"She's a lesbian." Andrea grimaced in expectation of her sister's response. Beth always called her on her bullshit, her smoke screens, and her half-truths.

"So?" Beth asked, surprising her. "You didn't hire her to sleep with the crew. You hired her to fix the problem, right?"

"Yes." Andrea noted that her sister had used almost the same words she'd used with Barry.

"Then what's the problem?"

Before Andrea had a chance to figure out what her answer would be, Beth jumped in. "Oh, my God, Andrea. You like her."

"What? I do not." She replied way too quickly. Beth knew when Andrea was lying, upset, or hiding something, and she often finished her sentences for her. Sometimes it was creepy and others downright irritating. They looked nothing alike, and other than sharing the same parents and birthdate, they were complete opposites. But sharing a womb had connected them like nothing else could, and even though her sister was a royal pain in the ass, especially at times like this, Andrea cherished her.

"You like this woman," Beth said again, seeming more confident in her deductive reasoning.

"Jesus, Beth, you make it sound like we're back in the sixth grade."

"Okay, you're attracted to her. You want to sleep with her."

"Now I think you've gone a little overboard."

"Have I?"

"Yes, you have," Andrea shot back but was unable to come up with any other substantial rebuttal.

"Then why are you struggling over her? You never have problems with your employees."

Beth was right; she never had any issues with the people who worked for her. They were all equally committed to the mission and knew what was expected. "Because I can't get her out of my control room."

Beth laughed.

"What?" Andrea asked. When had this conversation become funny?

"Did you just hear yourself?" Beth asked between laughs. "You can't get her out of your control room?"

"I know what I said," Andrea replied, probably a little too harshly, but she was tired and didn't have the energy or interest to try to figure out where Beth was going with this. "I can't fire her."

"Has she screwed up?"

"No."

"Are you afraid she might screw up?"

"No." And Andrea didn't want her to.

"Then suck it up, princess, and either figure it out or get over it."

"Jeez, Beth, people say I'm a hard-ass." Andrea couldn't help but laugh along with her sister this time.

"Speaking of hard asses, does she have one, or does she have a techno-nerd dough-body?"

Andrea and Beth went to the gym together three times a week, and both complained about how difficult it was to maintain their bodies. Beth was struggling to lose what she referred to as her baby-hibernation weight, and Andrea exercised because she sat behind a computer terminal all day.

"No." Andrea wondered just how firm Kenner's ass really was. Unfortunately, in her dream her hands never got there to find out.

"No, she doesn't have a hard ass or no she isn't a dough-body?"

"Beth, I have no idea what her ass feels like, or any other part of her body for that matter. And," she added, "I have no interest in finding out."

"Liar."

"For God's sake, Beth, let it go." How in the world could her sister know that her hands were tingling and her pulse racing from just talking about Kenner?

"She doth protest too much," Beth said.

"She is going to hang up now. Give my niece and nephew a big kiss from their Aunt Andi, and go fuck Paul until his eyes pop out of his head. Bye." Andrea heard Beth call her husband's name as she pushed the end button on her phone.

CHAPTER TWENTY

T-minus 03:14:57:14

Two days later, Barry and Mission Operations Director Grey entered the control room, and Andrea wondered what had taken them that long. The pressure from Barry, his boss, and the head of NASA was unrelenting. Ops Director Grey had been on her heels ever since he'd had to inform the top brass of the situation, and between that and the pressure Andrea had put on herself, she was ready to explode. They were quickly running out of time and were no closer to bringing home the crew than they were the day before.

The two men spent most of the morning hovering over each station, and her team wasted precious minutes answering questions nobody had time for. When they approached Kenner, Andrea braced for the worst.

She was too far away to hear the conversation, but if body language told her anything, the two men were none too happy. Kenner, of course, did nothing to help her cause. She barely acknowledged them, didn't move from her standard position of feet on the desk, keyboard in her lap, and gave what looked like one- or two-word answers to their questions. She never glanced away from her monitor.

Barry was about ready to burst. His fists were clenched behind his back, his posture ramrod straight, and the tips of his ears looked like they were on fire. When he started to look her way,

Andrea quickly made it appear she was studying a report. If she didn't make eye contact, maybe he would just go away.

Andrea had never minded when Barry was in her control room. As a matter of fact, she was proud of her team, their professionalism, and what they could do, and they were more often than not on shift when VIPs came in. But today was different. The clock was ticking, and it was getting louder and louder with each sweep of the second hand.

"Andrea, we'd like to speak to you," Barry said, his tone harsh, his words clipped. "In the conference room," he added just before turning his back on her and walking away.

Fuck. Andrea gathered up her notebook, the latest reports, and her pen. She felt, rather than saw, every set of eyes in the room on her back as she followed the two men out of the room.

Barry and Ops Director Grey were sitting next to each other on the same side of the table. She had no choice but to sit across from them. It was two against one and, as the Three Dog Night song said, one really was the loneliest number. She pulled out the heavy chair and sat on the edge of the seat, clasping her hands over the papers in front of her. She fought the natural urge to jump right in and start defending the work they had done up to this point, but she remained silent.

"Three days," Barry said, his voice flat. "We have three days until this becomes the biggest fuck-up in the history of NASA. And it will have your name all over it."

"And, it will be up to me to deal with the political and media fallout," Grey said.

Andrea sucked in a breath. She didn't need these two to tell her what she already knew. Did they think she hadn't already figured this out? Did she not think every second of every day that the lives of seven human beings were resting on her shoulders?

"Yes, sir, I'm certainly aware of that," Andrea was somehow able to say without gritting her teeth too obviously.

"What is Hutchings doing for us?" Barry asked. "Didn't look to me like she was accomplishing much of anything other than using our furniture for her personal lounge chair."

"Everyone is doing their best, sir," Andrea said, not bothering to look at Grey.

"You have three days, Andrea, or your best won't be good enough." The two men stood and stalked out of the room. They didn't close the door behind them.

Andrea left the conference room and walked calmly back to the control room. "My office, five minutes," Andrea said to Kenner's back before she strode away and back out the door.

"How about we grab a bite?" Kenner asked, stepping into her office. "One of the guys told me about a little place off Mercury Avenue that has the best..." Kenner stopped before finishing her sentence. "What? What?" Kenner repeated her question when she didn't answer.

Andrea couldn't believe it. They had three days to solve this problem, and Kenner didn't show even the slightest sense of urgency. Kenner's laid-back attitude and work style set Andrea's teeth on edge. Andrea had been working seven days a week, twelve and sometimes eighteen hours a day, while Kenner came in at seven and left just after the sun went down.

Andrea fought the urge to lash out at Kenner, but she was so tired she gave in. "Do you take anything seriously?"

"Excuse me?" Kenner asked, obviously confused.

"I asked if you take anything seriously. Anything at all. Just name one thing." Andrea held up a finger to emphasize her point.

"What are you talking about? Of course I take things seriously."

"Name one," Andrea shot back. She was getting angrier by the second.

"Andrea, what's going on here? Now why are you so pissed at me?" Kenner stepped into her office and closed the door behind her.

"Why? Why am I pissed at you?" This conversation was unbelievable. This day was unbelievable. This week was unbelievable.

"Yes," Kenner said, her voice rising. "I come in here and ask a simple question, and you bite my ass like I asked for the key to the executive toilet."

"That's exactly what I'm talking about."

"I have no clue what you're talking about," Kenner replied sharply.

Andrea rose from her chair and crossed her small office. She stopped inches from Kenner. "You think you can simply turn on your charm and coast on your reputation and—"

"Coast? You think I'm coasting?" Kenner turned serious and her eyes blazed.

"You haven't done anything meaningful since you got here. You waltz in here with your worn-out jeans, scuffed boots, and dazzling smile and charm the pants off everyone. They're so enthralled by you they can't see past the fact that you haven't done anything."

"You have no idea what you're talking about," Kenner replied, now almost shouting. "I've—"

"I know exactly what you've done, or haven't done, which is the more appropriate choice." Andrea pointed at Kenner to emphasize the word *exactly*.

"Don't point your finger at me." Kenner was almost growling by now.

"Or what?" Andrea knew she was intentionally antagonizing Kenner, but she couldn't help herself. Kenner made her so frustrated and angry she couldn't think straight sometimes. And this was definitely one of those times.

"Don't do this, Andrea," Kenner warned her.

Andrea ignored her and stepped even closer. They were so close Andrea could see the light-colored flecks in Kenner's dark eyes and feel her breath on her face. "Or what?"

Kenner snapped. She'd put up with a lot of shit from Andrea, and she'd had it. She grabbed Andrea's hand and twisted her arm behind her back. The sudden movement thrust Andrea's breasts against hers, and her mouth opened as she gasped in surprise.

Kenner had only intended to stop Andrea from poking her finger at her, but instantaneously her red-hot anger exploded into driving need.

She kissed Andrea, ravaging her lips, taking what she wanted. The tension between them had been growing and had finally exploded. With her free hand she grabbed the back of Andrea's neck and pulled her head even closer. For several seconds Andrea didn't move, and then just as suddenly she pressed her body against Kenner's and kissed her back with more want and desire than Kenner expected.

Heat shot through Kenner, and she let go of Andrea's hand as she spun her around and pushed her against her office door. She fumbled for the lock, and when she heard it click her clit throbbed. Kenner let her hands quickly roam over Andrea's soft body. She tugged on the buttons of Andrea's always impeccable starched shirt. She was so hot for her, wanted to feel and taste her skin so much, she ripped the few remaining buttons from the shirt. That seemed to be the only invitation Andrea needed, and she pulled Kenner's shirt over her head before returning her kiss her more savagely than before.

Pants slid to the floor, shoes were kicked off, panties and bras quickly discarded along with the stapler, picture frame, pencil holder, and half-a-dozen file folders from the top of Andrea's desk. Kenner sucked hard on one nipple, then the other as she quickly explored Andrea's body. Her senses took in everything as she discovered the wonder that was Andrea.

Her skin was smooth and soft in all the right places. Her skin tasted like sweat and sex, her nipples hard as pebbles in her mouth. Moans of pleasure reached Kenner's ears an instant after her fingers found warm, wet flesh. Kenner kissed Andrea again, her mouth and tongue exploring in rhythm with her fingers. Andrea wrapped her legs around Kenner's waist, her ass on the edge of her desk as Kenner's fingers dove in deep.

Andrea broke the kiss and wrapped her arms around Kenner's neck.

"Yes." Andrea moaned when Kenner flicked her thumb over Andrea's clit and her fingers slid into her. Kenner buried her face in Andrea's neck and bit down on the pale flesh below her ear. Kenner didn't know if Andrea was matching the rhythm of her fingers as she fucked her or if she was matching Andrea's, but it didn't matter. Andrea froze for a second, then smothered her cry in Kenner's neck. Andrea's climax flooded Kenner's palm, and she matched Andrea's pulsing orgasm with her own.

Before Andrea had a chance to recover Kenner was on her knees between Andrea's thighs, the burning need to taste her driving all sanity from her mind. Andrea leaned back and placed her feet on her desk, spreading her knees wide. Kenner didn't need any additional encouragement, and she replaced her fingers with her tongue.

"God, yes."

Andrea's words floated in the air around Kenner as she feasted on Andrea's most intimate place. She started with long, slow licks, which quickly increased in speed as Andrea responded. When her tongue darted in and out of Andrea's center, Kenner lost what little control she had left. Never had she wanted to please a woman like she wanted to please Andrea. She was completely consumed by Andrea's gasps of pleasure, the way her body arched closer to her mouth, the way she responded to her touch. Kenner slid her fingers in deep once again and sucked on the tight bulb of her clit. Andrea arched upward, pulled her head closer, and exploded again.

Andrea's head pounded in time with the rapid beat of her heart. Her breathing rate wasn't far behind as she struggled to catch her breath. Her brain was in a fog, the effects of hot sex dulling its normally quick thought process. She didn't move as she struggled to regain her equilibrium.

What the fuck had just happened? One minute she'd been pissed at Kenner and ready to throw her off the team, and the next Kenner had her fingers buried so deep in her Andrea could swear they were tickling her throat. Slowly, her eyelids heavy with fatigue, Andrea opened her eyes. The ceiling came into focus, and she felt something hard digging into her back.

The ceiling? Kenner's fingers? Oh my God, what just happened?

Andrea tried to think but was mortified. How to get out of this? How to get Kenner's finger out of her was more like it. How to regain some type of respectability was impossible to figure out while she lay naked on her desk with Kenner on her knees between her legs.

"Well, then." Kenner's voice was muffled, and Andrea felt her smile against her,.

Andrea shivered. Kenner's warm breath blowing on her wet clit when she spoke caused the involuntary reaction.

"You okay?" Kenner asked.

Andrea knew Kenner was looking at her, but she was so humiliated by her actions she couldn't bring herself to make eye contact.

"Yes," she replied stiffly. *Now do I wait for her to take her fingers out of me, ask her to, or reach down and do it myself? What a fucking mess.* Thankfully she didn't need to make that embarrassing decision, but she cursed her body when it shuddered as Kenner slowly withdrew. *Can this get any more awkward?*

As soon as Kenner stood, Andrea sat up and crossed her legs. She wanted to cover her breasts, but it was a little late for that now. A look of raw desire flashed in Kenner's eyes at her unintentionally provocative pose. Andrea quickly slid off the desk and began picking up her clothes. She stepped into her pants and stuffed her panties into the front pocket. She hastily donned her bra and shirt, tucking in the last few inches where the buttons were missing. She flushed with embarrassment when she remembered how desperately she'd wanted to have Kenner's hands on her.

"Andrea," Kenner said tentatively.

"You need to go." Andrea barely recognized her voice. It was husky from sex and her throat was dry.

"But…" Kenner began pulling her clothes on.

The last thing Andrea needed was to try to make conversation with Kenner. What in God's name did they have to say after this?

What had she gotten herself into? She never acted like this. She had never had sex with someone without knowing their favorite color or what flavor of ice cream they liked. And never, ever with someone she worked with. She didn't even want to think about the fact that it had happened at work. Holy shit! Someone could have heard them, could have walked in on them. The scenarios made her stomach turn, and for a moment Andrea was afraid she might throw up. That would be the perfect conclusion to an already humiliating, fucked-up situation.

"Just go," Andrea said, trying not to sound too demanding. "Please, just go." Her voice was almost pleading, and she willed herself not to look at Kenner. Please, please, please just go, she begged Kenner in her head. Finally, after what seemed like forever and three days, Kenner turned, unlocked the door, and left, taking all the air out of the room with her.

Andrea slid down the side of her desk to the floor. Drawing her knees up and wrapping her arms around them, she closed her eyes and dropped her head onto her arms. Twice. Twice in less than five minutes Kenner had made her come. The scent of her lingering arousal drifted up from her crotch. She shuddered, remembering the way Kenner had touched her, kissed her, licked her. Her head started to spin from the sensations. She tipped it back and took a deep breath to try to calm her racing heart.

What had she done? What had she allowed Kenner to do?

CHAPTER TWENTY-ONE

T-minus 03:14:22:10

Kenner turned into the nearest conference room, stepped inside, and locked the door behind her. Her legs shook as she crossed the room and pulled out a chair. She sat down and dropped her head on her forearms on the table. The scent of Andrea was still on her fingers and she inhaled deeply. Images of Andrea under her, pulling her closer, gasping her name as she came flooded her brain. Kenner's heart raced and her breathing was uneven. She'd had mutually satisfying quickies before but none that had left her as shaken as the one she'd just had with Andrea.

Kenner wasn't exactly sure how it had started, but touching Andrea had been nothing short of spectacular. She might have been able to stop before things had gone too far, but when Andrea had leaned into her and returned her kisses, there was absolutely no turning back. Their coming together had been intense and hungry, almost carnal.

Kenner sat up, her head spinning. Something strange and overwhelming washed through her, and her hands were still trembling. "What the fuck?" she said, rubbing her hands over her face. She groaned. The scent of Andrea was on her hands and face, and desire flared again. Jesus, that wasn't a good thing to do if she was trying to get her senses back. She'd never felt like this. After what she called a fast-and-furious fuck she always had simply felt sexually relieved and energized. Rarely had she wanted the woman again, and certainly not like she did with Andrea. She had to have her again and again, but the next time it would be slow and soft. The time after that fast and hard. Then standing, sitting, lying under her, kneeling over her.

"Jesus Christ, Kenner. Get it together," she said, standing up and beginning to pace back and forth beside the small table. "This is not good. This is not good at all." After a least a dozen laps, she exited the room and headed back to the control room.

Kenner wasn't paying attention, and when she rounded the corner into the ladies' room she practically ran over the custodian. "Excuse me," she said to the woman, who staggered back a few steps. She apologized again and checked to make sure the woman wasn't injured, then continued to the far sink. She cleaned herself up and laid a wet paper towel on the back of her neck. It didn't completely settle her, but it was better than nothing. She wet her hands again and ran them through her hair, looking at herself critically in the mirror.

Other than a light blush on her cheeks, she looked like she had before entering Andrea's office. In other words, perfectly normal. Inside, however, she was a mess. Two women talking and laughing entered through the double doors but both stopped when they saw Kenner at the sink. They quickly looked away and disappeared into adjacent stalls. Kenner took that as her cue to get back to the control room and tossed the paper towel in the trash on her way out the door.

❖

"Andrea?"

The rattling door knob startled her. Andrea had no idea how long she'd been sitting behind her desk or how she even got there. She barely remembered Kenner leaving. *Oh God, Kenner. Please let it not be Kenner.* She couldn't handle that right now, or ever.

"Andrea? It's Jackie. You in there? Barry said you were headed back this way."

Oh, fuck, that was the last thing she needed right now. Every company had their rumor mill, and NASA wasn't excluded from that drama. Jackie Grime was the main source of all that was gossip.

"I'm on the phone, Jackie," she was somehow coherent enough to say. She hoped that would make her go away.

"Why is your door locked?"

"I said I'm on the phone, Jackie," Andrea repeated, quickly picking up the items scattered on the floor and placing them back on her desk. She pulled out her desk drawer, frantically looking for a mirror. She knew she had one, but her hands were shaking so badly she couldn't find it. Finally, after her third time rummaging through the contents in the drawer, she pulled it out and held it up.

"Oh my God," she whispered. Anyone with any skill of observation would know she'd just been fucked. Her hair was a mess, her face was flushed, her lipstick nonexistent, and her eyes were glassy. She'd never had this look before. She ran her brush through her hair several times and re-secured it behind her neck. Somehow she managed to reapply her lipstick without ending up looking like a clown and took several deep breaths. The instant she stood up she remembered she was commando, pulled her panties from her pocket, and stuffed them into the zippered compartment in her briefcase. She knew Jackie was still outside her door and had no choice but to unlock it and hope she'd made herself at least presentable.

"Why was your door locked?" Jackie eyed her suspiciously.

"Because I didn't want to be disturbed," she replied, relieved that the handle on her door stayed locked even when opened from the inside. If Jackie had walked in on her with her hair a mess and her panties in her hand...Andrea shuddered as she silently imagined that scene.

"But you never lock your door," Jackie said, not so subtly looking over Andrea's shoulder into her office.

Andrea didn't have the time or the energy for her James Bond snooping. "Jackie, you have no idea what I do or don't do. Now, did you need something?" Andrea sounded harsh but didn't care.

"Yes. You're needed in the control room."

"Anything else?" Andrea watched Jackie pull her eyes away from the scan of her office and smile too sweetly.

"Nope, that's it."

Kenner felt, rather than saw, Andrea enter the control room. She didn't try to convince herself she wasn't waiting for her, but she was successful in not turning around to look at her. What was Andrea thinking? Was she as rattled as she was? Was she having difficulty focusing on what was in front of her? Was she reliving every moment? Every touch? Every sensation? Did she want more? Or was she mortified that she'd had pure, raw sex in her office? Was she chastising herself for losing control? Did she regret it? Was she embarrassed, ashamed,? Would she blame Kenner? Would she ever speak to her again or look her in the eye? Would she simply pretend it never happened? Was she experiencing the same emotional chaos over something she had no control over? Kenner wanted to look at Andrea, to somehow gauge her reaction, but she didn't dare, afraid of what she might see in Andrea's face, and she didn't like it that what Andrea thought mattered.

Minutes ticked by and hours dragged on, and she had no indication that Andrea was going to do or say anything to her. She knew Andrea hadn't left because her senses were still on high alert, as they were anytime Andrea was nearby.

"You need to go home, Hutchings. You look like shit," the man beside her said, stating exactly how she felt.

"Thanks, Saul, I appreciate your concern," she said sarcastically but with a smile. They had spent far too much time together these past seven days to be anything other than work BFFs. Kenner glanced at her watch, surprised it was almost nine.

After making a few notes on her pad and several dozen keystrokes, she stood, stretched, and started gathering her things. She tried to look behind her to Andrea's desk without being too obvious but only managed to catch a glimpse of an empty seat. Then she saw her from the corner of her eye talking to the propulsion specialist. Her body immediately responded to the memory of how Andrea's sighs had escalated into gasps, how her face had flushed with passion, and just how damn good she tasted, and she had to grab the back of her chair to steady herself.

She thought about interrupting to say good night, then thought better of it, then thought what the hell and headed their way.

The propulsion guy, whose name she didn't remember, looked her way first, and Kenner stepped next to Andrea when he stopped talking.

"I'm headed out," she said to no one in particular.

Andrea stiffened beside her and didn't acknowledge her in any way. When the silence among the three of them became awkward, Kenner turned and left the room.

CHAPTER TWENTY-TWO

T-minus 03:01:02:22

"You did what?"

"Beth, keep your voice down," Andrea said into her phone.

"Who's going to hear me? Paul and the kids are upstairs asleep, and I'm in the basement. Now tell me again what you did?"

"You heard me the first time, Beth. I don't need to repeat myself," Andrea said, just a little angrily. She'd had a hard-enough time saying it out loud in the first place.

"Oh, I heard you all righty, but I want to hear it again. I can't even begin to imagine—"

"Beth, stop it," Andrea said firmly. She didn't have to imagine anything. The scene kept playing in her brain over and over again, like a record with a scratch.

"Oh, all right, Andi. But you're no fun sometimes."

"Fun?" Andrea almost exclaimed. "I had sex…in my office… with an employee…a *female* employee." Andrea emphasized the word. "While seven of my crew members are stranded two hundred and fifty thousand miles away on the moon. On the fucking moon." It sounded too bizarre to be true, but Andrea was living the nightmare and knew it wasn't.

"Let's put the stranded crew members to the side for right now and focus on the sex, in the office, with a female employee. I assume we're talking about Kenner?"

"Jesus, Beth, who else would we be talking about?"

"No one, of course, Andi. I was just checking. You've been under a great deal of stress lately."

"And I'm going to have sex with a complete stranger in my office because of it? Get a grip, Beth." That's what Andrea needed to do—get a grip on the mess she'd just made. She'd tried to leave before Kenner did this evening, afraid she'd want to talk to her. She knew that was the coward's way out, but she had absolutely no idea what to say or how to act.

"So what happened?"

Andrea wished she had the answer to that question. "We were talking, and the next thing I knew we were…you know…" Andrea was waving her hand in the air like her sister could see it through the phone waves.

"No, I don't know, but I'd like to," Beth said, and in some other time Andrea could imagine them having this conversation after two bottles of wine while sitting on Beth's couch. As it was, she held a tumbler of scotch and was pacing in her living room.

"But we'll save that for later too. So what happened… after…?"

The word hung in the air, and the image that flashed in her head was definitely *during* and not *after*. Her clit began to throb again—or had it ever stopped?

"She left and went back to the control room."

"Just like that, she left and went back to work? I'm a little ill-informed on the lesbian hookup thing, but she didn't say anything to you?"

"You're asking me? I have no fucking clue on the protocol for something like this." Andrea refilled her glass and took another swallow.

"Okay, so, tell me exactly what happened. I doubt you two were just talking and she pounced. Or were you the pouncer?"

"No, I was not the pouncer," Andrea said firmly. She was a follower in bed, so her behavior shocked her in more ways than one. "She came into my office right after Barry had just reamed me out and asked if I wanted to get some lunch."

"I'll have to remember that line," Beth said jokingly.

"Beth, this isn't funny."

"I know, Andi. I'm sorry, but this is so unlike you. You're such a by-the-book Barbie, I never, in a million years, would have even imagined you would do something like that. I mean, I know you've had sex, but I never thought—"

"Can we stop talking about the sex part?" Andrea asked. "I have a serious problem I need to face tomorrow, and I have no fucking clue what to do." Andrea proceeded to explain to Beth the foreplay and afterglow of their encounter. An odd choice of words but true nonetheless.

"What do you want to do?"

Beth's question was so simple Andrea stopped pacing. What did she want? Her left brain was telling her she needed to apologize to Kenner for stepping out of bounds and that it in no way would negatively influence their working relationship. Yeah, that and Tuesday didn't come after Monday. Her right brain wanted to do it again. She wanted it fast, and hard, and completely without inhibitions. She wanted to feel her pulse race and her heart pound so hard she thought she would explode out of her chest. She wanted to gasp with pleasure and soar in the clouds of ecstasy. She wanted to taste Kenner on her tongue and hear her name whispered in the dark. She wanted to crawl under a rock and never come out.

"You can't avoid her forever, Andi," Beth said quietly, stating the obvious.

"Not forever. Just till we bring the crew home."

"Then what? Are you planning to ask her to dinner? Maybe see a movie or grab a cup of coffee? Exchange Christmas cards?"

Jeez, she'd called Beth for support and to help her figure out what to do, not be part of a comedy act. "Of course not, but my pressing problem is tomorrow morning." This is what Andrea had been dreading since Kenner had left earlier this evening.

"Well, it looks like you have several choices," Beth said. "You can act like nothing happened, apologize and tell her it will never happen again, resign because you feel you violated some inner code of conduct, or lock the door behind her and you pounce on her this time."

"Jesus, Beth, I'm so glad we had this chat and you helped me figure things out. It's late, go to bed. I'll talk to you in a few days."

Andrea dropped her phone on the couch and followed it, lifting her feet to the coffee table in front of her. She had fucked up. Seriously fucked up, and only she could get herself out of this situation. The problem was there was no manual or standard operation procedure for this one. She was in completely uncharted territory. She knew what she had to do but didn't know what she was going to do. When the clock on the wall behind her chimed one, she wasn't any closer to figuring it out.

CHAPTER TWENTY-THREE

T-minus 01:14:28:32

"So you're just going to ignore what happened between us," Kenner asked, her words a statement. Two days had passed since the incident in Andrea's office, and in that time Andrea had spoken to her only when absolutely necessary and never alone. Kenner had finally cornered her in her office after the morning briefing.

"Nothing happened," Andrea said, her eyes darting around the room.

"Nothing happened?" Kenner was surprised yet not surprised at all. She had expected Andrea would take the authoritative stance and demand that they simply brush it under the carpet, so to speak. "Then what would you call it? Because I remember something very definitely happened."

"A mistake."

"A mistake?" For some reason that word was like a jab in the stomach with a hot poker. It had been hard to have Andrea snub her for two days, but this was far worse. *This* was why she didn't get involved.

"Yes."

"You can't undo it, Andrea."

"Then I'll just pretend it never happened."

"Why?"

"Why?" Andrea asked, obviously confused by her question.

"Yes, why?"

"Your twenty questions are up. I don't have to answer that."

"Actually it's been only five. Why do you want to pretend it never happened? You can't just erase it like a program that didn't work or a standard operating procedure that's out of date." Kenner looked around Andrea's office—the scene of the "crime." Andrea didn't answer and Kenner pushed the point. "Why, Andrea? Are you afraid of what the answer might be?"

"Of course not," she shot back, her face reddening with anger.

"Then answer the fucking question."

"I am not going to dignify what happened or this entire conversation with an answer."

"Why? Because you liked it?" Kenner said, starting to get really pissed off. Andrea had clearly liked it, and Kenner wanted her to hear her say it.

Andrea stood, her face hard and angry. "How dare you?" she said through clenched teeth. Obviously Kenner had hit the right button.

"How dare I? You know, Andrea, there's a fine line between fighting and fucking."

"And you crossed it."

"I crossed it?" Kenner asked, stunned. That wasn't how she remembered it, especially when Andrea had grabbed her hair and raised her legs higher.

"Yes. This is a working relationship, not your latest hookup."

"I didn't hear you say no. As a matter of fact 'yes' came out of your mouth on more than one occasion. Especially when I was finger-fucking you and again when my tongue was on your clit."

"Get out," Andrea growled.

"My pleasure," Kenner said and started to leave. She stopped, tilted her head to the side, and said, "As a matter of fact, it was my pleasure, Andrea, and if you stop to admit it, it was yours too. We didn't commit a crime. Nobody forced anyone to do anything. We simply reacted to a situation in a natural, healthy way. And the sooner you admit that, the better off you'll be. Yes, you," she said, noting Andrea's shocked expression. "Because I'm perfectly fine with what happened."

Kenner stepped back and ran her eyes slowly over Andrea's body. Today she was wearing a pair of charcoal-gray trousers, her cuffs settling perfectly on her loafers, a crisp white blouse, and a gray-and-black checked scarf tied around her neck. She was stunning. All power and sensuality, and damn, she wanted her.

"Actually, I'm better than fine. And I'm not ashamed to admit I'd like to do it again. Maybe not right here," she said, motioning to her desk, "but somewhere else where we can take our time, not have to worry about anything or anyone except ourselves. So when you're ready, you know where to find me."

"Get out," Andrea repeated, her face flushed with anger.

❖

"I've got it!"

Every voice in the room stopped, and thirty-two pairs of eyes turned to look at Kenner, including Andrea's. She was standing waving a piece of paper in her hand.

"I've got it, I figured it out," Kenner said, her voice full of excitement and triumph. She looked around the room, her face glowing with accomplishment.

"What is it?" Andrea asked, stepping down from her desk area and weaving her way through the crowd to Kenner. The first thing she noticed was that Kenner looked tired, really tired. The second were the dark circles under her eyes, and the third, the sheer joy on her face.

"I figured it out," Kenner repeated. She went on to explain how she'd discovered the root cause of the ignition switches not firing and what the solution was. She answered dozens of questions shouted out from the people around her.

"Get it on the sim," Andrea said, referring to the flight simulator in the adjacent room. They would program Kenner's solution, then observe the shuttle's response.

Andrea tried not to be overly optimistic because many other simulations in the last few days had failed miserably. But this time was different. This time it was Kenner's solution, and Andrea had a gut feeling this one would work. Erring on the side of caution, she didn't plan to call Barry until they knew positively that it would succeed.

CHAPTER TWENTY-FOUR

T-minus 00:00:00:04

"Houston, we have ignition." Commander Albert's words resonated throughout the control room loud and clear.

A roar of jubilation erupted in the control room, reminiscent of the scene in the 1995 movie *Apollo 13* starring Tom Hanks when the command module broke through the re-entry silence after almost six terrifying days in space. Men and women were shaking hands and hugging as status lights that had been blinked red for ten days now turned green as each system powered up.

Someone was shaking Andrea's hand and slapping her on the back, but all she could see was Kenner. Actually, she could barely see her because of the celebratory crowd around her so thick it almost swallowed her. She'd come through for the seven astronauts and for this mission, and three hours and fifty-six minutes after Kenner had shot out of her chair, the engines fired up.

❖

The next three days were a hurricane of activity. While the crew was preparing for re-entry, Andrea's team still had work to do. They had systems to check, double-check, and triple-check. Coordinates to confirm, weather to forecast, recovery vehicles to move into place, and hundreds of other steps and procedures to complete to ensure the crew arrived home safely. The only contact she'd had with Kenner was after the daily meeting yesterday morning.

Everyone had been filing out like good little solders when Kenner had asked, "What has to be done for the crew to come home?"

Andrea studied Kenner for a moment, debating whether to give her the condensed or detailed version. She decided that Kenner would only be happy with all the information.

"Other than lift-off, re-entry is the most dangerous aspect of space flight," Andrea said. "Whereas on lift-off you're sitting on tons of liquid fuel, with re-entry you're traveling seventeen thousand miles an hour with the risk of burning up. So many things can go wrong."

"Walk me through it," Kenner said, but her request was really more of a question.

"The orbiter relies on gravity to bring it into the atmosphere so it's critical that it's turned and maneuvered into the proper position. Once the ship is in the right position, Captain Hight will fire the OMS, the orbital maneuvering system, which slows down the craft enough to enter the atmosphere," Andrea explained. "When and where the orbiter re-enters Earth's orbit is an exact science. It determines if they over- or undershoot the landing zone."

"Where does it land?"

"Sometimes back at Kennedy or at White Sands, New Mexico. Explorer will land at Edwards Air Force Base in California."

"What about the heat shields?" Kenner asked. Everyone who had ever heard of space flight knew about the most important part of the vessel. Unfortunately, its failure on the return of the shuttle Columbia *in 2003 had brought home its criticality after pieces of insulation from the external tanks fell off during lift-off, striking the wing of the shuttle. Unknown to anyone, the insulation had*

damaged the heat-protection tiles, and when Columbia had re-entered the atmosphere, hot gases had penetrated the damaged area and melted the airframe. The shuttle lost control and broke up above Texas.

"What about them? What are they made of?"

"Depends on where on the craft it is. Reinforced carbon-carbon is on the wing surfaces and underside, insulation tiles are on the upper forward fuselage and around the windows, Nomex blankets are on the upper payload bay doors, and white surface tiles cover the remaining areas."

Kenner had frowned in that certain way Andrea knew meant she was thinking something through. "Those materials have a high heat capacity," she finally stated.

"Yes, they do. Because the shuttle is moving so quickly into the atmosphere, it hits air molecules and builds up heat from friction."

"How hot does it get?"

"About three thousand degrees."

"Wow." Kenner nodded her understanding. "There's no radio communication during that time, right?"

"Right. The hot, ionized gasses surrounding the orbiter prevent radio communication."

"For how long?"

"About twelve minutes."

"Then what?"

"Once the shuttle hits the main air of our atmosphere, it's able to fly like a plane. At twenty-five miles from the landing zone, Commander Hight will assume control from the auto pilot and begin his descent. From then on it's wheels down, air brakes on, parachute deployed, and the shuttle slows to a stop."

"You make it sound so smooth, almost elegant."

Andrea's pulse tripped a beat or two at the intensity in Kenner's eyes.

❖

Static from the overhead speakers filled the control room already tense with anticipation. Andrea stared at the clock on the screen. The shuttle had been in communication blackout for eleven minutes, twelve seconds. Her outward calm appearance masked the inner turmoil that racked her. This was the critical stage of this mission, and until her crew was on the ground, she would not relax. These dozen minutes lasted an eternity, and the problems on this flight compounded the long wait even more.

"Twelve minutes, eight seconds into comm blackout," Capcom stated.

Andrea looked away from the clock and glanced around the room. Almost every man and woman was sitting on the edge of his or her chair, eyes glued to the large screen on the front wall. Those that weren't looking for any sign of the returning shuttle had their heads bowed in what looked like prayer. Andrea didn't much believe in God, but she'd take any assistance she could get to help ensure a successful end to this mission.

"Twelve minutes twenty-two seconds into comm blackout."

Andrea slowly stood, her heart racing. They had simulated this stage of the re-entry hundreds of times, and never had the comm blackout exceeded twelve minutes and fifteen seconds. Never.

Andrea's stomach seized as the seconds ticked by. Please, God, keep these men and women safe, Andrea said in silent prayer. She glanced at Kenner at the same time Kenner turned and looked her way. Their eyes met as if they were seeking reassurance from each other that everything would be all right.

"Thirteen minutes, four seconds into comm blackout." Capcom's voice wasn't as calm as it had been during his last readout.

Andrea couldn't pull her gaze away from Kenner. It was as if Kenner was her lifeline and to break that connection would break the fine hold she had on this mission, on her life. She didn't breathe and doubted anyone else in the room was taking a breath either.

The seconds ticked by, and a sense of dread started in the pit of Andrea's stomach and spread through her like molten lava. Fear tightened its grip around her heart. She felt dizzy and the room started to spin. All she could see was Kenner's face, her eyes communicating her own dread. This was the moment Andrea feared the worst, had nightmares about, that she would never forget. The crushing vise on her chest tightened.

The speaker crackled, and suddenly the strong voice of Commander Hight broke through like a rainbow after a hurricane.

"Houston, this is *Explorer*. How do you read?"

The response of Capcom was drowned out by the woops and cheers that were even louder than they were two days ago when the engines ignited. A huge smile broke over Kenner's face, and Andrea sat back down in her chair, her legs suddenly too weak to remain standing. She dropped her head in her hands and started breathing again.

❖

Andrea was finishing her report when she heard a knock on her office door. She'd had to close it an hour ago, the constant interruption of people stopping by to congratulate her too disrupting.

It couldn't be Barry, who was probably still on the phone with the president, ABC, CBS, and CNN. Supposedly he would appear on the morning news shows and a special edition of *Anderson Cooper 360°*.

"Come in," Andrea said, and when the door opened she immediately wished she'd ignored the knock. Kenner stood in her doorway.

"Got a minute?" Kenner asked tentatively.

Andrea hesitated. "Sure." Her heart skipped, then started racing when Kenner closed the door behind her. The last time they were in this room together they'd "talked" in a completely different language. Andrea didn't know if she could stop it if it happened again. She didn't know if she'd want to.

"We have to talk," Kenner said. She certainly didn't waste time with idle chatter.

"About?" Andrea knew her question was ridiculous, but she told herself if she acted like she didn't know what Kenner wanted to discuss, maybe the topic would be different.

Kenner scowled. "About what?"

Andrea leaned back in her chair, looking more relaxed than she was. Her stomach was cart-wheeling, her pulse racing, and her throat was dry. She was still processing the connection that had passed between them several hours ago in the control room. "Yes, about what?" It was almost as if she were challenging Kenner to bring it up. And they both knew what the *it* was.

Kenner looked around the room, her gaze lingering on her desk. Andrea knew Kenner was remembering what had happened there. As if she could forget. No matter how many times she wiped it down with a Clorox wipe, it still smelled like sex. God, what had she been thinking? She still couldn't believe what she'd done, what she'd let happen.

"If this has to do with anything other than this mission, it's not open for discussion."

"Why not?" Kenner asked, sitting in the chair across from her.

"Because we don't have anything to talk about. Your work here is done. You can go back and finish your vacation. I'm sure your company will let you."

"You and I have unfinished business."

"No, we don't."

"Yes, we do," Kenner said calmly, her eyes never leaving Andrea's.

"No, we don't."

"Did anyone ever tell you you're stubborn?"

"All the time."

"Too stubborn for your own good?"

"No."

"No?" Kenner asked, her eyebrows raising.

"I do what I need to do—"

"And you need to forget what happened between us?" She paused and looked pointedly to the desk. "Right here, on this very desk?" Kenner asked, her voice as soft as a caress.

"I don't need to forget it. I've just chalked it up to an unfortunate experience and have moved on." That was a big fat lie.

"Unfortunate experience?" Kenner asked, the expression on her face saying she knew Andrea was full of shit.

"Did you come in for something, or are you just going to mimic everything I say?" Andrea instantly regretted her question. She was trying to get Kenner out of her office, and now she'd just opened the door for further conversation.

"I was going to ask you if you'd like to go out to dinner," Kenner said.

Andrea read between the lines of Kenner's invitation. It had a completely different meaning than her previous "wanna grab a bite?" invitations.

"No, thank you."

"Why not?"

"I have a lot of work to do." Andrea's excuse was lame and she knew it.

"Baloney."

Jesus, Andrea hadn't heard that word since she was a kid. "I don't want to," she said simply.

Kenner didn't respond, just stared at her. Andrea wanted to look away or squirm under the intense eyes. Her palms itched to touch Kenner again, and her clit throbbed. "I don't think it's a good idea," she said finally.

"Why not?"

"Because you're leaving tomorrow." Why did Kenner keep asking questions? She'd made it perfectly clear.

"So?"

Kenner's one- or two-word questions were irritating her. "So? So you're leaving. Let's not pull any punches here, Kenner. You didn't ask me to dinner."

"I didn't?" Kenner asked, a slight smile curving her lips. The lips that not forty-eight hours ago had been on her most intimate places. She squeezed her thighs together and stifled a groan.

Andrea wanted to accept Kenner's invitation. No, it was really a proposition. She wanted to get lost in the feelings again. Even though that place where she lost control was frightening, she wanted to go there again. Wanted to feel like a woman. Desired, powerful, passionate. She was suddenly very tired of being the consummate professional, of working eighty hours a week building a career but having no one to share it with. Not that Kenner was the share-your-life-with kind of woman. She would be exciting, fun, an adventure Andrea would never forget.

But she was a coward, plain and simple. At least she was in her personal life. She'd always kept her personal and professional life completely separate. She had to in order to get where she was today. Sure, she'd finally arrived, but one mistake, one misstep, and she could be displaced in a nanosecond. Then what would she do? Her career would be ruined, and if, and it was a big if, NASA didn't fire her, she would be relegated to some administrative post far away from here. Even the thought of that possibility scared the shit out of her.

She had no idea what to do with someone like Kenner, and because of that, because she didn't fit into her neat little well-constructed world, she couldn't deal with her invitation. She didn't like change, didn't like things that she didn't know the outcome of, couldn't control the outcome. She was completely exhausted from the past several weeks. She had nothing more to give and certainly not even for one night with Kenner.

"Are we done?" Andrea asked instead of answering Kenner's question. "Because I think we are."

"And whatever you say goes, right?" Kenner suddenly turned angry. "Whatever Flight Director Finley says during the mission is the last word. Well, not this time, Andrea. This time I have the final word." Kenner stood. "Good-bye."

CHAPTER TWENTY-FIVE

T-minus 00:03:42:08

Andrea's hand shook as she handed her invitation to the tuxedo-clad man at the door. He was well over six feet tall and, based on his size, had probably played inside linebacker for some pro-football team. But his razor-short hair, earpiece cord twisting down the side of his neck, and his no-shit attitude gave him away as a secret-service agent.

The president had invited the crew and every member of Andrea's team to the White House for a formal celebration of the success of the mission. Last week the NASA press liaison had issued a mandatory meeting to discuss proper protocol while in the company of the president of the United States and the first lady. Andrea hadn't voted for the man, but because he was the president she had paid attention on the *do this* and *don't do thats* and the lengthy overview of the dress code.

Beth had insisted she go shopping, stating unequivocally, "No baby sister of mine is going to the White House in some out-of-date, off-the-rack dress." Andrea didn't even bother to fight that one, and when she'd looked in the mirror one last time before stepping out of her hotel room to take the elevator down to the waiting car, she didn't regret her decision.

Now she concentrated on putting one high-heeled foot in front of the other as she was escorted down a wide carpeted hall.

The walls were painted a deep shade of tan, contrasting beautifully with the artwork hung in perfect symmetry every six or eight feet. She heard no sound in the hall, but the sense of power and history seeped out of the walls. How many famous people had walked on these floors? Abraham Lincoln? Eleanor Roosevelt? Jackie Kennedy? Marilyn Monroe?

Andrea focused on the shoulders of the man in front of her. She didn't think he was a secret-service agent. He was too short, too thin, and too pasty. He must have been a butler or an aide of some sort. How did someone get a job like that? Was it passed down from father to son, mother to daughter? Did you go on employment.gov and fill out an application and then wait for the phone to ring? She imagined how odd that conversation would be.

"Good morning, Ms. Smith. This is Mr. Jones from the White House. We'd like for you to come in for an interview with the president. What does your schedule look like for next week?"

Andrea's thoughts were rambling, and she had to gain some type of control before she opened her mouth. She'd been a ball of nerves since receiving the invitation to this event three weeks ago. She'd finally admitted that she wasn't nervous because she was going to meet the president and the first lady but because Kenner would be there. The day before their flight to D.C., Barry had told her that Kenner's boss at Quantum had had to practically order her to attend. It was a conversation she'd never forget.

"I wonder if she'll bring a date," Barry said, using air quotes around the word date.

"I really can't say," Andrea replied, her stomach churning at the thought of another woman on Kenner's arm.

"I wonder if they'll dance."

Andrea detected more than a little slime in his comment. "And if they do?" Her response sounded like a challenge, and she didn't try to soften it with anything else.

Barry smirked. "That would be something to see, wouldn't it? Two qu...gays," he corrected himself, "dancing in the White House."

"It's lesbian."

"I know she's a lesbian," Barry said, frowning. "I'm the one that told you."

"Gay is used for men. Lesbian is the appropriate term for women. And you didn't have to tell me. I already knew."

"What do you mean, you already knew? Who told you?" Barry sounded like a kid whose secret had been stolen out of the bag.

"Because I know who's a lesbian and who's not."

"I can spot them a mile away too," Barry added, obviously desperate to be with the enlightened in-crowd.

"It's not always that obvious."

"What? Because you're a hero now and you have X-ray-vision eyes?"

When had Barry turned ugly? "No, I am not a hero." Andrea replied calmly. "Hundreds of people contributed to bringing the crew home."

"But you got all the glory. And now you're going to the White House."

So that was it, Andrea thought. Barry was jealous. Against her will she had been deemed the poster child of the mission, and she had hated every minute of it. She hated the photo shoots, the interviews, and the round of morning talk shows she was forced to attend. She always made it clear that it wasn't her but a team of people that deserved the praise and accolades.

"You're going too, Barry. It should be exciting," she said, trying to appease him. She'd been doing a lot of that lately.

"Big deal. All eyes will be looking at you, the first female flight director, and Hutchings and her gal-pal."

Andrea had never noticed until now how often Barry used finger quotes. It annoyed her.

"She'll probably wear a tux," he said, obviously disgusted with that possibility.

"So? It's definitely much more comfortable than a dress and heels." She'd thought of wearing one herself, but Beth had talked her out of it. Maybe she'd rethink that decision.

"So how can you tell if a woman is gay?" Barry asked like a dog with a bone. Did he have a drink or four at lunch? Andrea couldn't believe they were having this conversation. Sure, they'd run into each other at Target and were off the clock, but for Barry to talk like this? How had this man passed the psychological check? How did he pass the annual diversity-training tests? How had he not been drummed out of here?

"It takes one to know one," Andrea said, jumping off the come-out cliff in front of her.

The look on Barry's face was one of confusion, understanding, shock, and disgust.

"And before you say anything else, I'll remind you that I will crucify and ruin you if you say another degrading, demeaning word about Kenner or any other gay or lesbian you know, want to know, don't want to know, or that you even suspect is." She stopped to let her words sink in. "Do I make myself clear?"

Andrea almost ran into the back of the short, pasty man when he stopped in front of her. She needed to pay attention and have all her wits about her, as her grandmother used to say. She had no idea what exactly that meant, but everyone caught the gist of it. He opened the door and Andrea stepped inside.

CHAPTER TWENTY-SIX

T-minus 00:03:38:15

Andrea noticed the people immediately. Many she knew, even more she recognized, and she had no idea who a few of them were. Senator Marconi stood near the buffet talking with three men who looked familiar, but she couldn't put a name to any of them. They weren't from NASA so they must be other government officials. She didn't think anyone other than those related to the mission had been invited.

Flight Commander Jason Albert towered over the first lady to his left, and the first daughter, Rose, stood patiently beside her mother. Rose was taller than her mother and had her coloring, but she looked exactly like her father. A clone of the secret-service agent at the front door stood nearby. Music played softly in the background, and the subdued murmur of voices was occasionally punctuated with laughter.

Andrea felt eyes on her. It could have been any number of people, but when her skin started to burn and her nipples tightened she knew it was Kenner. She hadn't seen Kenner yet, didn't know if she was even here, but her body did. It sensed she was nearby and was preparing for her, already responding in anticipation of her touch, her taste, her scent.

Her hand trembled as she accepted a glass of champagne from a passing waiter. She wasn't a big drinker, but she definitely needed something to do with her hands. She took a sip and glanced to her left and froze. Kenner was looking directly at her, and even from across the room she could sense the heat in her eyes.

Real or imaginary, the music stopped and the room fell silent as Kenner's eyes traveled from her face, slowly down her body, and even more slowly back up again. Andrea couldn't breathe, her heart pounding so loudly in her chest she thought the tourists on the street could hear it.

Kenner was impeccably dressed in a dark suit with a teal-green shirt that would bring out the color of her eyes. Her hair looked freshly cut and lay neatly against her head. Andrea had an overpowering urge to walk over and mess it up, like it always had been every time she'd ventured into the control room. She was tall, stylish, hot, and Andrea wanted her.

The realization of the power Kenner had over her took her breath away. Her pulse roared in her ears with acknowledgement, a deep throb started between her legs, and her body tingled for Kenner's touch. My God, what was happening to her? She'd been in lust a few times. She knew the signs, but this response was traveling down a road she never knew even existed. Where had she been all her life to have missed this? Her nose had been in a book, her fingers on a keyboard, and her eyes on the screen in front of her. That's where she'd been, and suddenly she realized it had been a long and lonely road. Kenner started walking toward her, and Andrea felt herself leaning forward to meet her when a hand on her arm stopped her.

"Hey, Andrea. Can you believe we're actually here, in the White House?" Tony Douglas said with more than a little awe in his voice. "My daddy would probably box my ears to make sure I didn't do or say something stupid."

"I'll do it instead," his wife said, stopping beside him along with several other NASA employees. "The public-affairs lady drilled it into your heads to be polite and act like gentlemen, not the space jockeys you are," she said, referring to the nickname of the crew. She turned her attention to Andrea. "Andrea, your dress is beautiful."

Hearing her name, Andrea blinked a few times to clear her head. Her body, unfortunately, would take several hours to right itself, if she were lucky. "Thank you, Georgia. That's a beautiful color on you," she added politely, then looked at the copilot of the shuttle. "You clean up pretty good too."

"I can't seem to take enough showers," he said. "Fifteen days without one made me even hate myself, let alone anyone within eight hundred nautical miles of me." Everyone in the group laughed, and no one noticed that her chuckle was forced.

Andrea tried to follow the small talk in their group, but she tried even harder not to appear like she was looking for Kenner. She'd moved from where she'd been a few moments ago, that much Andrea knew, but other than that she was at a loss. She wanted to find her, go to her, talk with her, hear her laugh, see the sparkle in her eyes, feel her breath on her cheek.

But Andrea was afraid that when she did find Kenner, she wouldn't be alone. As far as Andrea could tell, everyone except her had come with a plus-one, and she assumed Kenner had as well. Kenner wouldn't care what the people in this room thought. She would bring whomever she wanted wherever she wanted, and if that upset anyone, they could just get over it.

"There's our magic worker," Tony said, extending his arm to someone approaching. Andrea knew it was Kenner without even looking. She took a deep breath.

Andrea had to stifle a gasp as a bolt of heat shot through her. Kenner surely saw it, and her already smoldering eyes flashed before growing darker. Andrea had seen those eyes before. She had seen them hovering above her, her back on her desk, looking up at her from between her legs, inches from her as she made her come against her office door. Oh God, she was going to either melt into a puddle or spontaneously combust if Kenner looked at her like that one second longer.

Tony introduced his wife before saying, "You here alone?"

Andrea tried to breathe but couldn't. She didn't want to know the answer to the question, so she quickly excused herself, saying she'd spotted someone she needed to talk to. She tried not to run away from the group, but Kenner's eyes on her back pushed her even faster.

"Ms. Finley."

Andrea stopped when the president stepped in front of her. He held out his hand. "Mark Cummings," he said, introducing himself like he was at any other party and not the host of the party in the most famous house in the world.

"Mister President," she said, acting on instinct. "It's a pleasure to meet you. Thank you for having us." God, she hoped she was as coherent as she thought she sounded.

"The pleasure is mine, Ms. Finley. I'm sure you felt the collective sigh of relief from the American people when the shuttle lifted off the moon, and mine was definitely one of them." The most powerful man in the world smiled at her. Was his expression genuine or well practiced?

"Yes, sir, we all did."

"I met Ms. Hutchings a few minutes ago."

The mere mention of Kenner's name sent a new round of sparks skimming through her body.

"Brilliant young woman," the president said. "She can talk circles around some of the best minds on my staff." The president looked over her shoulder, another smile forming on his face. He leaned closer almost conspiratorially. "Don't tell her," he said in a false whisper, "but I'm going to try to get her to come over to our side and work for her government."

"You're going to have to do some serious campaigning for that to happen, sir."

Andrea hadn't seen Kenner approaching from behind her, but now she caught a whiff of her cologne. Hundreds of images of Kenner flashed through her mind in the few seconds it took for Kenner to move beside her.

It had been a long time since she'd seen Kenner, the last time as she had exited the main gate seven weeks ago. She was even more stunning than Andrea remembered or fantasized in her dreams. Her eyes were sharp and piercing, giving one hundred percent of her attention to the person in front of her. Andrea had once been the focus of that attention, and she wanted to be again.

"I can be very persuasive, Ms. Hutchings. Just ask Congress. But not this week," the president said jokingly. "That group and I are working out some differences. But we'll get there. I just need to get them to see what I see, and that takes a little time. All good things come to those who wait, as my father used to say."

"Mine did too," Kenner said. "But as a kid I hated to hear it. I was never a very patient child. I'm still not as an adult, as a matter of fact. It gets me into a few jams now and then, but I seem to work my way out of them."

The president laughed. "Well, if you worked for me I could probably help you out of those jams," he said. "As long as they're not too big. I have several hundred million people watching me, you know."

"Yes, sir. I can imagine that could cramp your style."

Andrea was amazed at how easily Kenner and the president were joking with each other. It was like they'd been buddies in college and not the president of the United States and a young, brilliant scientist from Atlanta.

Kenner was finally alone with Andrea when the president excused himself. She was still reeling from seeing Andrea when she arrived. Breathtaking was the first word that had come to mind when she saw her across the room. Her heartbeat hadn't yet returned to its normal cadence, and her pulse was still racing. She took another sip of her water, her mouth still very dry.

Kenner had wanted to drop her drink on the nearest table, sprint across the room, grab her hand, and take her in the nearest secluded place possible. But Andrea was far too elegant, classy, and beautiful for a romp in the East Wing.

Kenner had known where Andrea was every second. She made the required small talk but had been looking for the right opening all evening to approach her. Finally, when it came, she'd acted like a tongue-tied schoolgirl on a first date.

God, she had to stop thinking like this. Andrea didn't want anything to do with her. She had made that perfectly clear on more than one occasion. She'd tried to forget Andrea in her work, her play, and in the arms of a few women. The first was somewhat successful, the second distracting to the point of danger, and the third a complete failure.

She'd always been able to lose herself in her work, and at times she was able to push Andrea out of her constant thoughts. But more often than not, a particular problem or the way she found herself sitting up straight in her chair brought Andrea back to the forefront of her mind. The still-healing scar on her chin attested to what could happen on the softball field when she'd been caught daydreaming instead of paying attention. And after not being able to touch two very naked and willing women, she'd stopped trying.

Andrea had gotten under her skin, in her blood, and inside every memory cell. Everything reminded her of Andrea. From the ringing of her phone in the middle of the night to a woman with thick, blond hair. She was afraid to sleep for fear of dreaming of Andrea, yet wanted to because that was the only way she'd ever be close to her again. Then came the invitation from the White House.

She hadn't intended to go. She didn't need to be reminded of what she couldn't have any more than she needed to have her right leg amputated. But when her boss found out, she'd had no choice, at least if she wanted to stay employed with Quantum.

Andrea's dress fell just above the knee and was classic in its design, complementing her curves. Kenner knew next to nothing about designers and fashion, but Andrea had clearly put herself together with care. Her dress floated around her as she walked, and Kenner itched to feel it against her cheek. Her heels were high, making her legs look like they went on for three days.

Kenner remembered them bent at the knee as she'd feasted on her. She wanted them wrapped around her waist, her leg, her head. God, anywhere on her body would be heaven. The weather in Washington, D.C. had been unseasonably warm, and Andrea's shoulders and arms were bare. Her hair was down, her jewelry understated but sparkling in the bright lights. A silver watch reflected the overhead lights, and up close her diamond earrings did the same. A light dusting of makeup and subtle eye shadow accentuated her beautiful face. Was the lip gloss as yummy as it looked?

She'd dressed carefully for tonight. The last thing she'd wanted to do was embarrass Andrea, especially in front of her boss, his boss, her employees and peers. She'd spent a small fortune on a haircut at a real salon instead of the small cookie-cutter shop in the mall. She'd set aside her boots and had spent another fortune on her shoes after the sales lady at Nordstrom had convinced her they matched the suit perfectly. Class and sophistication were her words, and the way Andrea looked at her now made it all worthwhile.

"How've you been?" she somehow managed to ask.

"Good, you?"

"Busy, but good."

"How is Atlanta?"

Andrea's accent set off a warm rush; she'd missed that Southern drawl. "Cold and getting colder every day."

During a long pause Kenner struggled for something to say. When they were together they were constantly sparring with each other, and now they could barely string two words together.

"You still solving all the problems of the world?" Andrea asked with a hint of a smile.

Kenner chuckled. "Hardly."

"What are you working on?" Andrea asked.

"Nothing special." No assignment would ever be special again. "You look incredible in that dress." Kenner let her eyes drift down Andrea's body, then back up again.

"Thank you," Andrea replied stiffly.

"Andrea," Kenner said. She had to say what was on her mind. She had to tell Andrea how she felt. How she couldn't stop thinking about her, how her body pulsed with desire for her, how she wanted to spend every day of the rest of her life with her.

"Kenner, don't," Andrea said, as if she could read her mind. "We've had this conversation, and I thought I made myself clear. I don't want to have it again, and certainly not here. Now, if you'll excuse me." Before Kenner could mount her offense it was Andrea's turn to walk away.

CHAPTER TWENTY-SEVEN

T-minus 00:00:08:18

Get out of the room, get out of the room. Andrea forced the cadenced message through her mind as she walked away from Kenner. Her legs felt like they were mired in quicksand, and it took all her strength to keep them moving. Unfortunately for her, it was time for the president's speech. An aide led her to a set of chairs on the dais, and she was seated far enough away from Kenner as to not have her in her line of sight, though not far enough not to be aware she was only a few yards away. But then again she was certain she would never forget the feel of Kenner.

Andrea had no idea how long the president spoke or what he said, and when she was told to smile for the camera, she did. It had been a long evening, and she was more than ready to go back to her hotel. She wanted to take off her dress, the one that made Kenner's eyes burn with appreciation and desire, step out of her shoes, the ones that made her legs look longer and more sexy than they actually were, and slide under the sheets, pull the blanket over her head, and not come out until the pain stopped.

She'd told Kenner no, that she wasn't interested. It had been the right decision at the time, and after almost two months it was still the right decision. But seeing her tonight had been almost unbearable. Andrea had lost track of how many nights she lay awake in her bed imagining Kenner's touch, her kisses, her fingers buried deep inside her. How many times had she relived those few short minutes in her office where her entire world had turned upside down? Those moments when she called Kenner's name in the darkness, her own fingers on her?

The room started to spin, and Andrea took several deep breaths to steady herself. It would not be good if she fainted right here in the East Room of the White House. She exchanged her empty glass of champagne with a full one as a waiter in starched white passed by. She shouldn't drink it; she'd already had one too many. She'd told herself to drink only water during this event, especially if Kenner was there. The last thing she needed to do was to lose what little was left of her control in a public setting like this.

The band had started playing shortly after the president spoke, and several couples were on the dance floor, including him and the first lady. They made a striking couple, and for a moment Andrea was envious of them. To be able to dance with the one you love anywhere, anytime without fear of public repercussions was something she'd never see in her lifetime. Not because gays and lesbians wouldn't eventually be accepted to the point that it wasn't a point at all, but because she'd never have someone to love. Not if she kept living like this.

In the days and weeks since the crew had returned, she'd thought a lot about what she'd worked for and what she'd given up to get here. She had few friends and even fewer lovers, and if it weren't for Beth, she probably wouldn't even have that. At times she felt like a social outcast. She didn't know who was on *Dancing With the Stars*, who'd won the World Series, or what an episode of *Breaking Bad* was like. Her bank account was full but her life was empty.

She slid unnoticed out the double doors onto the balcony. The lights of the capital city were twinkling in the night sky, like the stars overhead. She looked up and found the moon, the place that was the center of her greatest achievement. It was full and blindingly bright, and she remembered how she'd felt when Commander Hight had stepped onto its surface. Her heart had swelled with national pride and the fact that she was a part of history.

But lately she'd been in a funk, and she couldn't shake it. Beth said it was a natural letdown from the stress and excitement of the mission over the previous months. Beth had called it a "Okay, now what?" syndrome, which was the perfect way to describe how she felt. She was at loose ends. The mission she'd spent her life working toward was over. Now what was she supposed to do? How did you top that?

"Will you dance with me?"

Kenner's voice behind her startled Andrea, and she almost spilled her drink. She turned at the same time Kenner stepped into her line of view. "Excuse me?" She'd heard Kenner ask her to dance but needed a few more seconds to pull herself together.

"I asked if you will dance with me."

Kenner's direct, unwavering look took Andrea's breath away.

"I don't think so," Andrea replied carefully, shaking her head.

"Then don't—think about it," Kenner said at the obvious confusion on her face. She reached out and laid her hand on Andrea's arm. "I mean it, Andrea. Stop thinking about everything and just go with it."

Andrea's arm burned where Kenner touched her. Kenner made it sound so easy. Stop thinking, turn her brain off, and just go with what felt right. And she was certain dancing with Kenner would simply feel right. But it wasn't the right thing to do. Not here and not now. Actually nowhere and never was more like it. She could get mixed up and lost in Kenner Hutchings.

"Look around, Kenner. In case you've forgotten, we're at the White House at a party with the president of the United States, a dozen dignitaries, and four major television networks. Two women don't 'just go with it' and dance together."

"Why not? It's as good a place as any. As a matter of fact it's probably the best place. You know, 'land of the free, home of the brave' kind of place."

Kenner's quirky smile tripped her pulse. "Well, then you're a lot braver than I am, because outing myself in front of this crowd is not what I would consider a good time and an even worse career move."

"I'm not asking you to out yourself. Just dance with me." Kenner's voice was soft.

Andrea looked at Kenner like she'd just lost her mind. "I know you're smarter than that, Kenner. Two women don't dance together because they like the song."

"Why are we doing this, Andrea?"

"What?" Andrea asked, confused over the shift of the conversation. "Why are we doing what?"

"Pretending we don't want to rip each other's clothes off and fuck each other until we drop."

Heat tore through Andrea at Kenner's words and the image they evoked. Wasn't that what they'd done in her office? And didn't she want to do it again? Even if her brain said no, her subconscious said yes as it relived it every night.

"I have to go," she said hastily, desperately needing to get away from Kenner before she succumbed to her desire for her.

"Going to run away again?"

Andrea's back stiffened. She'd never run away from anything in her life. "What do you want from me, Kenner? Another fast and furious fuck on a desk?" Andrea looked around. "How about the table over there?" She pointed across the patio for emphasis. "Or over there in the corner? That looks dark enough that no one would see us."

"Andrea—"

"If that's what you want, then you'll have to find it someplace else. One of the servers can't keep her eyes off you. I'm sure she'd have a go with you. Now if you'll excuse me," Andrea said and started to leave. She didn't get far before Kenner grabbed her arm.

"Do you hate me that much?" Kenner's expression hardened.

"What?" That was the last thing she'd expected Kenner to say.

Kenner didn't answer her question. "That you can't do or say anything nice or decent to me? The competition for smartest woman in the room is over, Andrea. I won because I solved your problem. You won for bringing me in to solve it. It's a tie, a draw, a stalemate, or whatever you want to call it. But it's over." Kenner stepped back a bit and looked at Andrea, comprehension dawning on her face. "Or maybe you just don't like me."

"Don't be ridiculous," Andrea said. "I don't hate you. I never did."

"Then what is the problem?"

Andrea had no idea where this conversation was going. She didn't know how it even got started. The pattern of confusion and uncertainty that always centered around Kenner hadn't stopped just because she'd left NASA grounds. Andrea still had a hard time focusing, her dreams continued to have Kenner as the main character, and a haze of anxiousness seemed to follow her around.

"What do you want from me?" Andrea asked, not certain if she really wanted to know the answer.

"I've changed my mind," Kenner said. "I don't want to dance with you right now."

Andrea instinctively knew that whatever Kenner did want was more powerful than a simple dance.

"I want to kiss the most beautiful woman in the most famous house in the world," Kenner answered softly.

❖

Kenner's eyes burned with heat, and it coursed through Andrea's body down to her toes. No one had ever called her beautiful. No one had ever looked at her the way Kenner was gazing at her now. No one scared her like Kenner did.

Kenner's eyes never left hers when she spoke. "I am going to count down from three, Flight Director Finley, and when I get to one, I intend to kiss you. So you have a choice here, Andrea, and you have three seconds to decide."

Andrea's heart leaped, her pulse skyrocketed, and nothing existed in the world except her and Kenner right here, right now. She wanted to kiss her, feel her soft lips on hers, taste her again.

Kenner continued to look directly into her eyes. "Three." Kenner started to lower her head. "Two." Andrea's heart beat faster, her mind whirling with indecision. "One."

The kiss was electric. Kenner's lips were soft and warm as they glided over hers. Kenner deepened the kiss, and when Andrea opened her mouth, the kiss turned blinding. Andrea struggled to not lose her mind as Kenner's tongue explored her. She tasted like whiskey and a hint of garlic. She smelled like sunshine and summertime. And when Kenner pressed her body to hers, Andrea felt like she'd just come home.

Andrea wrenched away, covering her mouth with her hand. She gasped to catch her breath, her head spinning. Kenner was looking at her, her expression one of confusion and disbelief. "I have to go," Andrea said shakily and almost ran off the balcony and back into the main room.

Kenner watched Andrea hurry away. She wasn't sure what had just happened. Shit, from the moment Andrea had glided into the room tonight she hasn't been sure what had happened. When Kenner saw Andrea she couldn't look anywhere else but at her.

Kissing Andrea had been like magic. She'd offered Andrea the opportunity to step away, and when she didn't, Kenner knew her luck had changed. Her lips were warm and sweet and, after a second's hesitation, eager. When she'd deepened the kiss, Andrea's mouth had opened and Kenner could swear she heard her moan. Andrea's tongue had battled hers for control, or was she feasting on Kenner like Kenner was devouring her? It didn't matter. What did matter was that when Andrea put her hands in her hair that was the only invitation Kenner needed to press her body against her.

Andrea had molded herself to her, slightly shifting so that Kenner's leg was pressed against her crotch. The tight dress had prevented any closer contact, but when Andrea had thrust her hips forward in an attempt to get closer, Kenner had responded in kind. Her kisses had become more aggressive, and her hands had started to wander. She'd dragged her lips from Andrea's to explore her smooth neck, then trailed back up again to claim her luscious mouth.

Kenner was on fire. Her heart raced, her pulse hammered in her head, and she was overcome by desire for Andrea. Their attraction was like spontaneous combustion, and they had been seconds away from doing just that. Her hands drifted lower, and when they met the cool flesh of Andrea's thighs, she'd almost lost it. She'd forced herself to hold it together but almost lost it again when she started to inch Andrea's dress up and Andrea had surged into her again.

"Andrea," Kenner had whispered against her neck as she slid her trembling hand under the dress to caress her hip. When she'd shifted to gain better access, Andrea had wrenched herself away, one hand covering her mouth, the other pulling her dress down. It took Kenner several seconds to realize what had just happened. Andrea was breathing fast, her face flushed with arousal and something else Kenner couldn't identify.

"Andrea?" Kenner asked softly, moving closer. She'd stopped when Andrea stepped back, a look of shock and fear on her beautiful face.

"Don't do that again," Andrea said, her voice shaking. "I have to go." She'd turned and disappeared into the main room.

It took Kenner several minutes to pull herself together enough to reenter the festivities. The crotch of her briefs was wet and her face felt flush, a testament of how much she wanted Andrea. No way could she walk back into that room looking and feeling like this. But Andrea had, and Kenner wondered how she'd done it.

❖

Somehow Andrea made her excuses and her exit without embarrassing herself. Barry was talking to Senator Marconi, who'd been sucking up to the president all night. Most of the crew was still in attendance, as was most of her staff. It looked like the event would go on for several more hours, but it would have to go on without her.

A car was waiting to take her back to the hotel, and when she slid into the backseat and fastened her seat belt, she realized just how exhausted she was. She'd been a nervous wreck ever since receiving the invitation, not only because of the venue and the host but because she might see Kenner again. But she'd never thought she'd kiss her again. Certainly not a kiss that rocked her world like that one just had.

She had practically thrown herself at Kenner without thought of where they were or that any number of very important people could have walked out on the balcony expecting a breath of fresh air and gotten something much more than that. Her career would have been ruined if that had happened. Everything she had sacrificed, had worked and dreamed for, would collapse right before her eyes, dissolve just like she had in Kenner's arms.

What had come over her? She hadn't been herself since the shuttle ignition problem began. But who could blame her? First her astronauts were stranded, and then Kenner had arrived and thrown her nice, calm, well-planned mission into total turmoil. And what Kenner did to her was something she still didn't understand.

Kenner brought out the worst in her, and Andrea didn't like it. Never before had she lost focus. Never before had she lost concentration. Never before had she lost her temper. Never before had she had sex in her office. Never before had she almost had sex in the White House. The White House, for God's sake. Never before had she felt like this. Had she completely lost her mind?

She just needed to get back home and return to her life. She had reports to write, a magazine that wanted to do a feature on her, and the next mission to plan for. She would be leading that one as well, and even though it was two years away, she still had plenty to do.

The car door opened and Andrea stepped out into the warm Washington night. She took a moment to admire the lights from the Lincoln Memorial and the Washington Monument, then turned away from the hotel's front door. She was keyed up and knew sleep was impossible. Maybe a walk would help settle her.

The streets were crowded with bustling tourists and workers in the nation's capital heading home from another long day at the office. Fanny packs and cameras outnumbered briefcases and wingtips, and Andrea stayed to the inside of the sidewalk so as not to impede those who were moving faster than she was.

She meandered down the street, passing entrances to other hotels and restaurants, with no destination in mind. A professional-looking couple strolled along in front of her, their arms interlocked, their shoulders touching intimately. By observing the way their bodies moved together, so familiar and comfortable, Andrea knew they were lovers. The sound of their laughter drifted behind them to her, and a pang of envy jolted her.

How had this couple met? Who asked the other out first? Who made the first move for a kiss, their first touch, their first sigh of passion? How had they managed to have both a career and what appeared to be a very fulfilling personal life? Did either of them fear where their relationship might lead? Obviously they weren't afraid to take the risk. How did people get to be that way? She couldn't remember ever wanting to take a risk in her entire life. How had that happened? Was it her DNA? Had something happened as a child that she didn't remember? Had she just not encountered a risky situation? Had her life always been boring and sedate?

The couple side stepped into a darkened doorway of a closed coffee shop, where they wrapped their arms around each other and kissed. It wasn't a groping, tongue-sucking kiss, but it was definitely a prelude to what would come later. Was that what she and Kenner had looked like on the balcony earlier tonight? Did their bodies mold perfectly together like they were made for each other? Did they have the same sense of unspoken urgency for more?

She couldn't go on like this. Kenner was on her mind all the time. First she couldn't wait to get rid of her, and now, weeks later, all she wanted to do was see her again. She wanted to listen to her rapid-fire questions, experience her quick mind and sharp comments. To hear her laugh, see her face light up when she smiled. But how could she do that when she'd made it clear to Kenner she didn't want that? God, what a mess her life was. Andrea turned around and headed back to her hotel.

Chapter Twenty-eight

T-minus 00:00:09:02

Kenner was sure Andrea wouldn't answer the door, and because of that she didn't know why she was even here in the first place. Andrea had made it very clear that she wasn't interested, whether it was for another quickie or anything else. So why was she continuing to stand here moments away from getting kicked in the gut...again?

In the endless seconds that ticked by, the events of the last two months came into focus. She had spent most of her adult life on the prowl. Sex cleared her mind, relaxed the tension that had built up, and just felt good. Damn good. So why not? It was a natural bodily function that God made as an important feature in life. Not having sex was like not going to the bathroom. Everything that came into her body, whether it was food or the stimulation of a beautiful woman, had to come out somehow. To keep it all bottled in was just not healthy. And she did her part to be as healthy as possible.

Until the job at Quantum came along she'd drifted from company to company, growing uninterested in a matter of months. Quantum offered her variety and something puzzling to challenge her every day. She bored easily and thrived on the unknown and where the next assignment or person she met would take her. After the disaster with Eva, she had intended to never get serious with anyone. If you cared, then you could be hurt, and Kenner had definitely no interest in that. She had been all about light and casual, never staying in one place too long. But Andrea had changed all that.

From the first moment Kenner saw her walk into the conference room she'd been fascinated with her. Sure, Andrea was a woman in a traditionally man's world, but so was she. So what? She'd gotten over it and obviously so had Andrea. Andrea was uptight, and Kenner wanted to see her loosen up. Andrea was serious, and Kenner wanted to see her laugh. Andrea was cool, almost to the point of being cold, and Kenner wanted to watch her melt, wanted to make her melt.

In the beginning it had been a challenge to prove to herself she could rattle Flight Director Finley's chain. Then it became a contest of wills, the scaling of a vertical wall that Kenner was not about to lose. She didn't always intentionally antagonize Andrea, but sometimes she just couldn't help herself. Andrea was a challenge to be conquered, a mystery to be solved, a puzzle to put together. But their roles had reversed, and Andrea had scrambled her mind when she'd reached for Kenner in her office. That, she would never, ever forget.

"Andrea." The thick door muffled Kenner's voice. "I know you're in there. Don't try to hide from me." She knocked again, this time louder. "Andrea, open the door."

Andrea opened the door, not wanting to cause a scene in the hall. Kenner stood there looking dashing, elegant, and confident all poured perfectly into her impeccably cut suit. Andrea's heart started banging against her ribs, and her legs felt weak. Kenner was powerfully attractive and Andrea was definitely affected by her appeal.

Neither of them spoke. Andrea felt the caress of Kenner's look as her eyes moved up and down her body. Her nipples tightened and her stomach tingled. The heat between her legs matched the heat in Kenner's eyes.

Andrea wanted to know how Kenner had found her, but a woman like Kenner could probably charm information out of anyone. It thrilled and rattled her that she would make the effort. It also scared the shit out of her so she instead she took the offensive. "Did you come here for a reason or to just stand there in the hall?"

Andrea's sharp words seemed to snap Kenner out of her blinding stupor. "Yes, I'd love to come in. Thanks."

Andrea tried to block the doorway but Kenner slipped by. "I didn't invite you in," Andrea said as she passed.

"Close the door. It's Washington. Gossip flies around here like leaves in the fall." Kenner walked farther into the room. "Nice place," she said, glancing around the room. It was large, with a small couch, two sitting chairs nearby, and a king-sized bed at the far end. "Mine isn't nearly this big," she observed.

"What do you want, Kenner?" Andrea was obviously exasperated at her being here.

Kenner thought for a moment before answering. Why was she here? Was it the challenge she'd made for herself to crack Andrea's cool exterior? Was it the way she lost complete control when Andrea had kissed her? The small act of surrender when Andrea pulled her closer? Because she wanted to know every dip, hollow, curve, and bend of her body? Because for the last seven weeks she couldn't get Andrea off her mind, and that never happened with a woman? Or was it because Andrea made her feel things that scared her and thrilled her at the same time. Kenner heard the wheels turning, felt the shift of a decision and a rush of calmness flow through her as she started to speak.

"I want to learn your favorite color, see you in your favorite pair of jeans and what you wear when you wash the car. What's your favorite cake to have on your birthday? Hell, when is your birthday? I want to know if you wear funny PJs to bed and laugh in the rain. I want to know how much you love your mother and hate broccoli. I want to learn what's up here," Kenner said, tapping her left temple. "And I want to learn what's in here." She laid her hand over Andrea's heart, which was racing. "I want to know what turns you on. To discover what makes you quiver with desire, and I want my name to be the only one you cry out because of it. I want to learn everything about you."

Andrea couldn't move. She couldn't process the words Kenner had just said. They were totally unexpected. She'd expected more smart-aleck comments and sarcasm, not this. Not…oh my God… what was she saying?

"You light up my life like nobody else has. You fill places in my heart I didn't even know I had. I want to feel your heart beat against me. I can tell by the way you kiss me, Andrea, that we have something between us."

"What?" That was all Andrea was able to say, and that itself was difficult. What was Kenner talking about? Was she talking about her? Other than the one fling, they'd been at each other's throats the entire time Kenner was on her team. How could she be thinking like this? "You can't be serious?" Andrea asked, moving away from Kenner. With Kenner that close and her eyes that dark, Andrea couldn't think straight. Hell, she could barely think at all.

"I know, Andrea. I'm scared shitless too."

"That's not it. We barely know each other."

"I know enough," Kenner said, seeming as calm as Andrea was nervous.

"You…we…" Andrea stammered, not sure what she was trying to say. "We practically killed each other…before." Kenner's smile sent another shock wave through her.

"There's a fine line between love and hate."

Now she was completely stunned. Love? Hate? What in the fuck was happening? One minute she was barely making conversation with Kenner, and the next she had her tongue down her throat followed by her telling Kenner never to do it again. Apparently Kenner hadn't listened because she was standing in her hotel room looking at her with those eyes. The ones that made her stomach flutter, her blood burn, and her heart stutter.

This turn of events had shifted so fast her head was spinning. First, she hadn't wanted Kenner in her control room, and then she'd kept looking for her. She'd poked and prodded and antagonized her, hoping she'd leave, but she'd pulled Kenner closer when Kenner took her in her office. She'd told her to go and thought only of her after she did. She'd come to this party hoping to avoid Kenner, yet secretly wanting to see her again. She reached for the chair behind her and sat down.

"You live on the other side of the country." Andrea said the first thing that came into her mind.

"It's only three states and a two-hour plane ride."

"We're too different."

"They say opposites attract." Kenner countered her easily.

"I stay between the lines. You don't even have any lines," she said anxiously.

"I'll stay wherever you are." Kenner's eyes were steady on hers.

"I need calm, routine, predictability. You're flash, give-and-go...spontaneous." Andrea knew she was grasping.

"I can't promise routine, but I can promise you I'll be there for you every second of every day."

Andrea's mouth fell open and then closed several times, her arguments empty. Kenner was still standing where she'd stopped when she came into her room. She radiated confidence

"I'm ten years older than you." Even to Andrea, that one sounded pathetic.

"It's not like I'm fifteen and you're twenty-five."

"You look fifteen," Andrea said, and her stomach flip-flopped when Kenner's face grew serious and she slowly started toward her.

"I'm a grown woman, Andrea. I've made my own decisions for years. I'm brilliant and remember every word of every conversation I've ever heard. I remember how you said yes when we were together. I remember how your body spoke to me when you were in my arms. I remember how I felt when you kissed me."

Kenner stopped in front of her, and Andrea had to tip her head back to look at her. Kenner's eyes blazed.

"I know what I want, Andrea. And it's you."

The intensity in Kenner's eyes, the firm set of her jaw, the sheer magnetism of her standing mere inches away made Andrea freeze.

Kenner took her hand and pulled her to her feet. "I'm going to count down from three, and when I get to one," Kenner said, repeating the warning she'd given Andrea an hour ago.

"You're going to kiss me," Andrea said.

Kenner's face split into a wide grin, her eyes sparkled, and she nodded. "I'm going to kiss you."

Kenner's simple statement took Andrea's breath away. Her body vibrated, her heart thumping so loud Kenner had to hear it. She dropped her eyes to Kenner's mouth as she counted down.

"Three…"

Kenner's voice was soft and her head dropped closer, their breath mingling. Andrea quivered with anticipation, heated from Kenner's confident words and actions. This was what she wanted. What had filled her dreams for weeks. What had filled her heart. She wanted Kenner's lips on hers, on her breasts, on that hot, throbbing point between her legs. She wanted Kenner to take her, wanted to give herself completely to Kenner. No regrets, no holding back. *This* is what she wanted—Kenner's insatiable desire for her. She needed Kenner to touch her in a way no one else had and that no one else ever could, that no one else ever would. Andrea reached for Kenner before she had a chance to say the next number.

CHAPTER TWENTY-NINE

T-minus 00:00:00:00

The instant their lips met, Andrea gave up. She gave up fighting what she didn't understand. Gave up holding back emotions she'd never experienced before. Gave up her carefully choreographed life. She gave up everything to simply feel.

Kenner's lips were soft, her moans enticing. Her shoulders were strong, the fabric of her suit jacket rich and smooth. Her breathing was getting faster, her heart pounding. She smelled wonderful, a mixture of cinnamon and fresh air, and Andrea breathed her in like this was her last breath.

Her hands trembled as she slid the suit jacket off Kenner's shoulders and down her arms. It fell to the floor with a soft whoosh, and as soon as Kenner's arms were free she wrapped them around Andrea's waist. Kenner's mouth continued to plunder hers, and Andrea was beginning to feel light-headed. But she needed more—much, much more. Desperate to feel her, Andrea tugged on the buttons of Kenner's shirt. She whimpered, frustrated that they weren't opening as fast as she needed them to be.

"Hey," Kenner said, covering her hands with hers. "It's okay, slow down. We've got all night."

Kenner kissed her softly this time, and when she pulled her head back, she was smiling that quirky smile that always made

Andrea's stomach flip-flop. "Unless there's someplace else you'd rather be?"

"As a matter of fact, there is," Andrea replied, bolder than she'd ever been. Taking Kenner's hand, she crossed the room and stopped beside the king-sized bed. She pulled down the duvet, exposing the crisp, white sheets underneath. Andrea closed her eyes and took a deep breath, gathering her courage. When she opened them and turned around, Kenner was waiting for her to make the next move. Andrea thought her intentions were pretty clear, but when Kenner hesitated she suddenly doubted herself.

"At the risk of losing my butch card and embarrassing myself, I have to admit I'm more than a little nervous," Kenner said.

"Nervous?" Andrea was instantly relieved. "If anyone should be nervous it should be me."

"Well, I've never made love to someone I'm crazy about before. Talk about performance anxiety."

There it was again, that smile, and instead of engaging in another debate with Kenner, Andrea simply said, "You make me crazy. But I'm crazy about you too." She reached for Kenner again.

Kenner's entire body trembled in anticipation of Andrea's touch. Her skin burned where Andrea touched it as she unbuttoned her shirt. Kenner wanted to copy her movements, eager to feel Andrea's skin on hers, but she let Andrea set the pace. This time neither of them would have any regrets. They wouldn't have any doubts about what was happening between them.

When Andrea pulled her camisole over her head, cool air hit Kenner's nipples, already hard with yearning to feel Andrea's skin on hers. This was right, more right than anything she'd ever thought could be.

Kenner kept her eyes glued to Andrea's hands as the back of her fingers caressed her stomach, then slid open her belt buckle and opened the top button. Her pulse pounded in her ears when Andrea started to pull her zipper down, and Kenner had to clench her fists to keep from speeding up the process. What felt like days later, Andrea's hand completed its agonizingly slow descent and stopped right where Kenner really, really needed it to be. She couldn't hold back a moan when Andrea pressed her fingers there.

"You're killing me." Kenner groaned, clenching her teeth together for control. When Andrea lifted her head, the look in her eyes took Kenner's breath away. It showed pure, raw hunger, and Kenner almost came right there.

Andrea didn't take her eyes off hers as she slowly slid Kenner's pants down off her hips. Her stomach tightened at the sound of her belt buckle hitting the floor. What that sound symbolized was unmistakable. Andrea took a small step backward, her eyes roaming over Kenner's naked body. Everywhere she looked, Kenner felt the heat of her gaze, and by the time Andrea spoke, she could barely stand.

"You are incredible."

"You have far too many clothes on," Kenner somehow managed to choke out, her voice sounding nothing like it normally did.

Andrea's smile was mischievous. "You're the master problem solver," she said, clearly fighting a smile, her innuendo containing a challenge. "Fix it." She knew Kenner never walked away from a challenge.

THE END

About the Author

Julie Cannon divides her time by being a corporate suit, a partner, mom, sister, friend, and writer. Julie and Laura, her wife, have lived in at least a half a dozen states, traveled around the world, and have an unending supply of dedicated friends. And of course the most important people in their lives are their three kids.

With the release of *Countdown* in October 2015, Julie will have thirteen books published by Bold Strokes Books. Her first novel, *Come and Get Me*, was a finalist for the Golden Crown Literary Society's Best Lesbian Romance and Debut Author Awards. In 2012, her ninth novel, *Rescue Me*, was a finalist as Best Lesbian Romance from the prestigious Lambda Literary Society, and *I Remember* won the Golden Crown Literary Society's Best Lesbian Romance in 2014. Julie has also published five short stories in Bold Strokes Anthologies. www.JulieCannon.com

Books Available from Bold Strokes Books

Break Point by Yolanda Wallace. In a world readying for war, can love find a way? (978-1-62639-5-688)

Countdown by Julie Cannon. Can two strong-willed, powerful women overcome their differences to save the lives of seven others and begin a life they never imagined together? (978-1-62639-4-711)

Heart of the Liliko'i by Dena Hankins. Secrets, sabotage, and grisly human remains stall construction on an ancient Hawaiian burial ground, but the sexual connection between Kerala and Ravi keeps building toward a volcanic explosion. (978-1-62639-5-565)

Keep Hold by Michelle Grubb. Claire knew some things should be left alone and some rules should never be broken, but the most forbidden, well, they are the most tempting. (978-1-62639-5-022)

The Courage to Try by C.A. Popovich. Finding love is worth getting past the fear of trying. (978-1-62639-5-282)

The Time Before Now by Missouri Vaun. Vivian flees a disastrous affair, embarking on an epic, transformative journey to escape her past, until destiny introduces her to Ida, who helps her rediscover trust, love and hope. (978-1-62639-4-469)

Twisted Whispers by Sheri Lewis Wohl. Betrayal, lies, and secrets—whispers of a friend lost to darkness. Can a reluctant psychic set things right or will an evil soul destroy those she loves? (978-1-62639-4-391)

Deadly Medicine by Jaime Maddox. Dr. Ward Thrasher's life is in turmoil. Her partner Jess has left her, and her job puts her in the path of a murderous physician who has Jess in his sights. (978-1-62639-4-247)

New Beginnings by KC Richardson. Can the connection and attraction between Jordan Roberts and Kirsten Murphy be enough for Jordan to trust Kirsten with her heart? (978-1-62639-4-506)

Officer Down by Erin Dutton. Can two women who've made careers out of being there for others in crisis find the strength to need each other? (978-1-62639-4-230)

Reasonable Doubt by Carsen Taite. Just when Sarah and Ellery think they've left dangerous careers behind, a new case sets them— and their hearts—on a collision course. (978-1-62639-4-421)

Tarnished Gold by Ann Aptaker. Cantor Gold must outsmart the Law, outrun New York's dockside gangsters, outplay a shady art dealer, his lover, and a beautiful curator, and stay out of a killer's gun sights. (978-1-62639-4-261)

The Renegade by Amy Dunne. Post-apocalyptic survivors Alex and Evelyn secretly find love while held captive by a deranged cult, but when their relationship is discovered, they must fight for their freedom—or die trying. (978-1-62639-4-278)

Thrall by Barbara Ann Wright. Four women in a warrior society must work together to lift an insidious curse while caught between their own desires, the will of their peoples, and an ancient evil. (978-1-62639-4-377)

White Horse in Winter by Franci McMahon. Love between two women collides with the inner poison of a closeted horse trainer in the green hills of Vermont. (978-1-62639-4-292)

The Chameleon by Andrea Bramhall. Two old friends must work through a web of lies and deceit to find themselves again, but in the search they discover far more than they ever went looking for. (978-1-62639-363-9)

Side Effects by VK Powell. Detective Jordan Bishop and Dr. Neela Sahjani must decide if it's easier to trust someone with your heart or your life as they face threatening protestors, corrupt politicians, and their increasing attraction. (978-1-62639-364-6)

Autumn Spring by Shelley Thrasher. Can Bree and Linda, two women in the autumn of their lives, put their hearts first and find the love they've never dared seize? (978-1-62639-365-3)

Warm November by Kathleen Knowles. What do you do if the one woman you want is the only one you can't have? (978-1-62639-366-0)

In Every Cloud by Tina Michele. When she finally leaves her shattered life behind, is Bree strong enough to salvage the remaining pieces of her heart and find the place where it truly fits? (978-1-62639-413-1)

Rise of the Gorgon by Tanai Walker. When independent Internet journalist Elle Pharell goes to Kuwait to investigate a veteran's mysterious suicide, she hires Cassandra Hunt, an interpreter with a covert agenda. (978-1-62639-367-7)

Crossed by Meredith Doench. Agent Luce Hansen returns home to catch a killer and risks everything to revisit the unsolved murder of her first girlfriend and confront the demons of her youth. (978-1-62639-361-5)

Making a Comeback by Julie Blair. Music and love take center stage when jazz pianist Liz Randall tries to make a comeback with the help of her reclusive, blind neighbor, Jac Winters. (978-1-62639-357-8)

Soul Unique by Gun Brooke. Self-proclaimed cynic Greer Landon falls for Hayden Rowe's paintings and the young woman shortly after, but will Hayden, who lives with Asperger syndrome, trust her and reciprocate her feelings? (978-1-62639-358-5)

The Price of Honor by Radclyffe. Honor and duty are not always black and white—and when self-styled patriots take up arms against the government, the price of honor may be a life. (978-1-62639-359-2)

Mounting Evidence by Karis Walsh. Lieutenant Abigail Hargrove and her mounted police unit need to solve a murder and protect wetland biologist Kira Lovell during the Washington State Fair. (978-1-62639-343-1)

Threads of the Heart by Jeannie Levig. Maggie and Addison Rae-McInnis share a love and a life, but are the threads that bind them together strong enough to withstand Addison's restlessness and the seductive Victoria Fontaine? (978-1-62639-410-0)

Sheltered Love by MJ Williamz. Boone Fairway and Grey Dawson—two women touched by abuse—overcome their pasts to find happiness in each other. (978-1-62639-362-2)

Asher's Out by Elizabeth Wheeler. Asher Price's candid photographs capture the truth, but when his success requires exposing an enemy, Asher discovers his only shot at happiness involves revealing secrets of his own. (978-1-62639-411-7)

The Ground Beneath by Missouri Vaun. An improbable barter deal involving a hope chest and dinners for a month places lovely Jessica Walker distractingly in the way of Sam Casey's bachelor lifestyle. (978-1-62639-606-7)

Hardwired by C.P. Rowlands. Award-winning teacher Clary Stone, and Leefe Ellis, manager of the homeless shelter for small children, stand together in a part of Clary's hometown that she never knew existed. (978-1-62639-351-6)

No Good Reason by Cari Hunter. A violent kidnapping in a Peak District village pushes Detective Sanne Jensen and lifelong friend Dr. Meg Fielding closer, just as it threatens to tear everything apart. (978-1-62639-352-3)

Romance by the Book by Jo Victor. If Cam didn't keep disrupting her life, maybe Alex could uncover the secret of a century-old love story, and solve the greatest mystery of all—her own heart. (978-1-62639-353-0)

Death's Doorway by Crin Claxton. Helping the dead can be deadly: Tony may be listening to the dead, but she needs to learn to listen to the living. (978-1-62639-354-7)

Searching for Celia by Elizabeth Ridley. As American spy novelist Dayle Salvesen investigates the mysterious disappearance of her ex-lover, Celia, in London, she begins questioning how well she knew Celia—and how well she knows herself. (978-1-62639-356-1)

The 45th Parallel by Lisa Girolami. Burying her mother isn't the worst thing that can happen to Val Montague when she returns to the woodsy but peculiar town of Hemlock, Oregon. (978-1-62639-342-4)

A Royal Romance by Jenny Frame. In a country where class still divides, can love topple the last social taboo and allow Queen Georgina and Beatrice Elliot, a working class girl, their happy ever after? (978-1-62639-360-8)

Bouncing by Jaime Maddox. Basketball Coach Alex Dalton has been bouncing from woman to woman, because no one ever held her interest, until she meets her new assistant, Britain Dodge. (978-1-62639-344-8)

Same Time Next Week by Emily Smith. A chance encounter between Alex Harris and the beautiful Michelle Masters leads to a whirlwind friendship, and causes Alex to question everything she's ever known—including her own marriage. (978-1-62639-345-5)

All Things Rise by Missouri Vaun. Cole rescues a striking pilot who crash-lands near her family's farm, setting in motion a chain of events that will forever alter the course of her life. (978-1-62639-346-2)

Riding Passion by D. Jackson Leigh. Mount up for the ride through a sizzling anthology of chance encounters, buried desires, romantic surprises, and blazing passion. (978-1-62639-349-3)

Love's Bounty by Yolanda Wallace. Lobster boat captain Jake Myers stopped living the day she cheated death, but meeting greenhorn Shy Silva stirs her back to life. (978-1-62639-334-9)

Just Three Words by Melissa Brayden. Sometimes the one you want is the one you least suspect. Accountant Samantha Ennis has her ordered life disrupted when heartbreaker Hunter Blair moves into her trendy Soho loft. (978-1-62639-335-6)

Lay Down the Law by Carsen Taite. Attorney Peyton Davis returns to her Texas roots to take on big oil and the Mexican Mafia, but will her investigation thwart her chance at true love? (978-1-62639-336-3)

Playing in Shadow by Lesley Davis. Survivor's guilt threatens to keep Bryce trapped in her nightmare world unless Scarlet's love can pull her out of the darkness and back into the light. (978-1-62639-337-0)

Soul Selecta by Gill McKnight. Soul mates are hell to work with. (978-1-62639-338-7)

The Revelation of Beatrice Darby by Jean Copeland. Adolescence is complicated, but Beatrice Darby is about to discover how impossible it can seem to a lesbian coming of age in conservative 1950s New England. (978-1-62639-339-4)

Twice Lucky by Mardi Alexander. For firefighter Mackenzie James and Dr. Sarah Macarthur, there's suddenly a whole lot more in life to understand, to consider, to risk...someone will need to fight for her life. (978-1-62639-325-7)

Shadow Hunt by L.L. Raand. With young to raise and her Pack under attack, Sylvan, Alpha of the wolf Weres, takes on her greatest challenge when she determines to uncover the faceless enemies known as the Shadow Lords. A Midnight Hunters novel. (978-1-62639-326-4)

Heart of the Game by Rachel Spangler. A baseball writer falls for a single mom, but can she ever love anything as much as she loves the game? (978-1-62639-327-1)

Getting Lost by Michelle Grubb. Twenty-eight days, thirteen European countries, a tour manager fighting attraction, and an accused murderer: Stella and Phoebe's journey of a lifetime begins here. (978-1-62639-328-8)

Prayer of the Handmaiden by Merry Shannon. Celibate priestess Kadrian must defend the kingdom of Ithyria from a dangerous enemy and ultimately choose between her duty to the Goddess and the love of her childhood sweetheart, Erinda. (978-1-62639-329-5)